This book belongs to

....

CONTENTS

Edited by Mara Alperin. *Designed by* Pritty Ramjee.
Cover illustrated by Stuart Trotter.
Endpapers illustrated by John Harrold.

THE
RUPERT®
ANNUAL

EXPRESS NEWSPAPERS

EGMONT
We bring stories to life

Published in Great Britain 2017 by Egmont UK Limited
The Yellow Building, 1 Nicholas Road, London W11 4AN
Rupert Bear™ & © Express Newspapers & DreamWorks Distribution Limited.
All Rights Reserved.

ISBN 978 1 4052 8757 9
67238/1
Printed in Italy

No. 82

RUPERT

Rupert and Bill run free as air
Till something makes them stop and stare.

"Hey, Bill Badger! Look at that!" Rupert's pal Bill Badger breaks off from the race the pair are having high on Nutwood Common and points. Sticking out of a nearby tree stump is an arrow. But it's no ordinary arrow, as the pals discover when they get close. It is made of shiny metal, it's big and it is making a humming sound. As long as it's buzzing neither of them feels like touching it.

and the BOOMERARROW

A gleaming arrow's what they've found
Which makes a curious humming sound.

Although it's stuck fast in a tree,
Together they can pull it free.

Then suddenly the sound stops. The pals wait a little then Rupert says, "Shall we try to get it out of the stump?" Bill nods. So Rupert has a go at freeing it. It won't budge. Bill tries. Just the same. Then Rupert grasps it, Bill holds him round the waist, they tug – and out it comes. "I say, it's a beauty!" breathes Rupert. "I wonder how it got here and whose arrow it can be."

"A beauty!" both the friends agree,
"But whose," asks Rupert, "can it be?"

John Harrold.

RUPERT TRIES OUT THE ARROW

Before surrendering his find
Rupert first has some fun in mind.

"Let's fire the arrow from my bow,
I wonder how far it will go?"

Bingo's amused by this new sport
But scoffs as both their shots fall short.

"The bow's too small, that's what's amiss,
You'll need a stronger one for this!"

Well, plainly the arrow belongs to someone so, of course, Rupert and Bill decide the right thing to do is hand it in to PC Growler, Nutwood's village bobby. "But there can't be any harm in our having a go with it first," Rupert grins. So back the pair go to Rupert's cottage where Rupert fetches out his small toy bow. It makes the arrow seem even bigger. He is fitting it to the bow when another of his pals, Bingo the clever pup, turns up.

Neither of the others notices him until he gives a snort of laughter at Rupert's attempt to fire the big arrow. "You'll never fire it with that teeny bow!" he scoffs. "Here, let me try," says Bill. "I'll show you!" But his effort is no better and Bingo laughs even louder. "If you're so clever . . ." Rupert begins. "Oh, I am," chuckles Bingo. "But not with a toy bow. Come to my house and I'll show you." So off the three troop.

RUPERT'S PAL WANTS TO TRY IT

Their chum has something they must see,
He's interested in archery.

"I'm not the only one!" he adds,
"It's one of the Professor's fads."

And now with pride the clever pup
Reveals a gadget he's thought up.

"Before we fire this bow of mine,
We'll tie the arrow to some twine."

Everyone in Nutwood thinks of Bingo as "the clever pup" because he is forever inventing and making things. Not all work, but quite a lot do. On the way to his place he confides, "This arrow's just what I've been looking for." "Oh, you mustn't keep it!" protests Rupert. "We were going to take it to PC Growler when we'd tried it out. He'll find out whose it is." "I'm pretty sure whose it is," smiles Bingo as they reach his workshop. "The Professor's!"

The Professor is a clever old man who lives with a servant in a tower near the village. "He and I are competing to see who can make a machine to launch an arrow the farthest," says Bingo as he throws open the door. "Here's mine! My electric crossbow! I haven't made an arrow yet so we'll try it out with the Professor's. And just to make sure we don't lose it as he seems to have done . . ." He reaches down from a shelf a long coil of stout twine.

"This arrow's too sharp!" Rupert calls,
"It might hurt someone when it falls."

Such problems don't stump Bingo though.
He's got the answer, you might know!

"An old sink plunger!" Rupert cries,
"A perfect fit!" the pup replies.

While Bill helps Rupert tie a knot,
Bingo prepares to fire the shot.

As Rupert and Bill help him to move his machine outside, Bingo explains that one end of the twine will be tied to the arrow, the other to something firm here. "But we can't just fire it anywhere," Rupert points out. "It's too sharp. It might hurt someone." "You're right!" says Bingo and disappears indoors to reappear with the sort of rubber plunger you use for unstopping blocked sinks. "Now what's he up to?" gasps Bill.

"An old sink plunger!" Rupert exclaims. "What for?" Bingo's answer is to remove the plunger's handle and fit the rubber part over the arrow's point. "A perfect fit!" he grins. "Just like those toy sucker ones that stick to the target." Now, while Rupert ties the twine to the arrow, Bingo gets the machine ready. A battery motor draws back the bowstring. He pulls a knob. "This holds the bowstring in position," he says. "I just move it back to fire the arrow."

RUPERT FINDS HIMSELF FLYING

"The crossbow's ready, looking fine!
Here, Rupert! Just secure the line!"

Then Bingo turns and cries, "Oh no!"
He's accidentally fired the bow . . .

Not ready for this sudden flight,
Poor Rupert gets an awful fright.

Too late to let go, he's so high,
He's yanked at top speed through the sky.

The electric crossbow is ready. The bowstring is drawn back and locked in position by one of the knobs. Bingo fits the arrow into his machine. "Here, Rupert," he calls. "Fix this line to something firm. That clothes pole will serve." Rupert takes the coil of twine across to the clothes pole, looking for a good place to tie it. In the same moment Bingo turns to talk to Bill and his smock catches the firing knob. "Oh, no!" he cries as the bowstring slams free.

Bingo's warning cry comes an instant too late. Rupert, reaching for the clothes pole, doesn't see what's happened and he is still clutching the coiled line as the arrow is fired. Before he knows what's going on he is yanked off his feet. Bill and Bingo stand frozen in horror. By the time they can catch their breath to shout "Let go!" Rupert is far too high to do that. All he can think is, "This can't be happening to me! Oh, that Bingo and his silly machine!"

RUPERT SEES DANGER AHEAD

Frightened to give a downward glance,
He hangs on tight and trusts to chance.

He's sure he'll crash, beyond a doubt.
But no! The arrow levels out.

Propelled by some unusual power,
It veers to the Professor's tower.

"The arrow's his!" Rupert decides.
Then dead ahead a huge bird glides.

Up, up streaks the arrow with Rupert clinging desperately to the coil of twine. He daren't look down and all the time through his mind go the words "What goes up must come down – and, oh, that's me!" That moment must come soon. But no! Instead of plunging back to earth the arrow levels out. After a moment Rupert risks opening his eyes. The arrow is flying level, but faster than ever! And above the rush of air he hears the arrow buzzing loudly again.

As the buzzing restarts the arrow changes direction, heading across Nutwood village towards . . . what? Then Rupert sees what – the tower home of the Professor. Of course! Since it's his arrow he must somehow be controlling it. And, yes! There he is! On the roof. "He'll get me out of this," Rupert hopes desperately. But at that very moment a huge bird flies right into the path of the arrow. "Get out of the way, stupid thing!" Rupert yells.

12

RUPERT IS CARRIED AWAY

The two must hit! They must collide
Unless the creature moves aside.

The bird – a courier for its King –
Snatches the arrow and its string.

Then, catching Rupert round the waist,
It bears him off in angry haste.

"Come back!" the old Professor pleads
But on its way the great bird speeds.

Nothing, it seems, can stop the arrow hitting the bird. Rupert's shouted warning has no effect. He sees the Professor shouting too. Then in an instant the great creature seems almost to brake in mid-air and the arrow passes harmlessly in front of it. In the next instant the bird has swooped and snatched the arrow in its beak. Braked like that, Rupert starts to tumble, but even as he does he recognises the bird!

It is the Courier, the messenger, of the King of the Birds. He doesn't fall far. The Courier drops and catches him. To his surprise – when he can think again – he finds the bird's grip surprisingly gentle. That's all very well, but what's the creature going to do with him? On the roof of the tower he can see the Professor calling and beckoning to the bird to land. But the huge thing ignores the old man and carries Rupert away from Nutwood.

As he looks down now Rupert sees
Peaks and lakes and scattered trees.

At last they near the journey's end,
Home of the Bird King – Rupert's friend.

The mighty bird comes to a halt
And drops poor Rupert with a jolt.

The creature's still upset, it seems,
And fills the air with angry screams.

Soon Nutwood is left far behind. The land below becomes wilder yet to Rupert it is somehow familiar. Then he remembers. Of course! It's on the way from Nutwood to the Kingdom of the Birds! And that makes Rupert feel better, for more than once his adventures have led him to that strange place. He has even met the Bird King and been able to help him, so he feels sure the King will understand that he meant no harm to the Courier bird and send him home.

Now the palace of the King of the Birds appears through the clouds. The Courier glides towards one of its many terraces, hovers just above it and lets go of Rupert so that he lands with a nasty bump. Then it lands beside him, drops the arrow from its beak and lets loose a series of ear-splitting angry screams. Poor Rupert has to cover his ears. Plainly the huge creature is still very upset about its near miss with the arrow.

RUPERT IS LOCKED UP

In answer to its raucous shout,
A courtier and guards rush out.

"Dangerous flying is the charge,
This bear cannot be left at large!"

Rupert is marched across the yard,
On either side there stalks a guard.

"Now lock him in here while I fetch
The Chamberlain to judge the wretch!"

In answer to the Courier's screams two of the palace guards appear with a very pompous-looking bird courtier at their heels. At once the Courier starts to squawk what clearly is a complaint. As it listens the courtier looks more and more serious and when at last the Courier finishes it addresses Rupert: "You are in trouble! Dangerous flying, but even worse, interfering with a Courier on the King's business."

Then it snaps an order at the guards who prod Rupert to his feet and start to march him away. "You've got this wrong!" he protests. "Be quiet!" snaps the courtier. "The Courier does not tell lies!" The little party halts at last beside a large birdcage which one of the guards unlocks. "In you go and wait while I fetch the King's Chamberlain," the courtier orders Rupert. "As the King's chief minister he is the one who must decide what is to be done with you."

15

And then without another word,
Off struts this very pompous bird.

"The King alone can hear this trial
He won't be back for quite a while."

So Rupert's carried off to wait,
Perhaps for weeks, to learn his fate.

Just then a curious plane draws near.
His friend the old Professor's here!

The arrow is put into the cage with Rupert, the cage is padlocked and off struts the courtier to fetch the Chamberlain. When the two return they look stern, but the Chamberlain's first words cheer Rupert up: "Your offence is so grave only the King may deal with you!" And, of course, that's what Rupert wants, believing that the King will understand he meant no harm. But the Chamberlain goes on, "However, the King is away on a trip and may not be back for weeks."

"You can't mean to keep me here until he comes back!" Rupert wails. "My Mummy and Daddy don't know where I am!" But all that happens is that the courtier orders the guards to bring the birdcage and follow it. So, slung on a pole, Rupert's birdcage prison is carried to a terrace on top of a high tower. Just as they arrive Rupert hears the drone of an engine. He looks up, and there is the strange little aircraft of his friend the Professor!

RUPERT'S FRIEND TURNS UP

Although he doesn't mean them harm,
The birds all scatter in alarm.

"No planes allowed!" they crossly squawk.
"Please!" says the old man, "Let me talk."

He tells them he's come specially
To ask them to set Rupert free.

"He's not to blame for that near miss,
For I controlled his flight with this."

Rupert is overjoyed at the sight of the Professor's aircraft. But he's the only one on that high terrace who is. The birds' open-beaked astonishment at its sudden appearance gives way to panic and they scatter as it lands. Then fear is replaced by anger when the engine stops and the Professor climbs out smiling. Hopping up and down with rage, the courtier squawks, "No planes allowed! How dare you bring that thing here of all places!"

"Please let me explain!" pleads the Professor. "I know you must dislike flying machines in your lovely kingdom but it's the only way I could get here to explain that Rupert is in no way to blame for the accident that almost happened to your, er, colleague. You see, I was testing my boomerarrow and somehow Rupert got caught up by it." He goes to the aircraft and takes from it a strange device. "I was, in fact, controlling the boomerarrow's flight with this."

RUPERT'S FRIEND HAS TO GO

"My boomerarrow's something new,
An arrow that comes back to you."

The Chamberlain won't change his mind,
Rupert, he says, must stay behind.

Reluctantly the old man goes,
He'll get no further here, he knows.

He calls to Rupert, "Hold on tight!
Don't worry, it will be all right."

The birds don't look at all impressed, but the Professor presses on: "I call my invention the boomerarrow because I can make it return like a boomerang – with this." Once more he indicates the device he is holding. "It got stuck somewhere while I was testing it –" Rupert nods. But the Professor is not allowed to go on. "Enough!" the Chamberlain cries. "I do not understand a word you say! The plain fact is this bear was flying with a dangerous arrow which almost put paid to the King's Courier and he must await the King's judgement. Now leave at once!" The birds look so fierce that the Professor backs towards his machine and climbs in. Rupert's heart sinks. But before the old man starts his engine he calls to Rupert, "Don't worry. It will be all right. But stay alert." Then he starts the engine and the aircraft rises. But above the noise Rupert is sure he hears him yell, "Hold on tight!"

RUPERT HEARS A SOUND

But as the aircraft disappears,
Rupert is very close to tears.

"The King dislikes all aeroplanes.
He'll be so cross!" a bird exclaims.

Imprisoned on a windswept tower,
Rupert grows glummer by the hour.

Then suddenly he pricks his ears,
What is that strange new sound he hears?

Dismally Rupert watches the Professor's aircraft disappear. He's so upset that he doesn't think about what his old friend said before leaving. He can only think about having to stay cooped up in this cage until the King of the Birds returns. Nor is he any happier hearing the Chamberlain say as the birds leave him, "The King will be so cross about the bear's friend bringing his aeroplane here. He dislikes the noisy things intensely."

Rupert can't remember ever having felt so miserable, caged, alone on a windswept tower. At least his parents will learn from the Professor where he is. Then he recalls the old man's parting words. "Stay alert." Not much chance of doing anything else in this wind. But what did he mean? And why did he shout, "Hold on tight"? Just then, above the whine of the wind, Rupert hears another sound – from something very close at hand.

RUPERT'S CAGE IS TOWED AWAY

A buzzing noise, there's no mistake,
The boomerarrow starts to shake.

The cage begins to rock apace
Until it topples into space.

The birdcage plunges through thick cloud
The buzzing now is really loud.

Out from the cloud he comes to find
He's left the birds' realm far behind.

In fact the new noise is coming from the boomerarrow. It has started to buzz again. Now the buzzing grows and the boomerarrow shakes as if trying to break free. The cage lurches towards the edge of the tower. Rupert grabs at the boomerarrow's tail meaning to untie the line and let it away. But in that second two things happen: He sees what the Professor meant by telling him to "stay alert" and "hold on tight" – and the cage topples into space!

For an awful moment Rupert is sure that the cage is plunging out of control. Then he realises that it is really being towed by the boomerarrow through the clouds on which the Bird King's palace stands. Above the swish of the air he hears the boomerarrow buzzing louder than ever. Suddenly they break out into brilliant sunshine and Rupert sees how far above the earth they are – and that they are still diving!

RUPERT IS RESCUED

The arrow levels, then it streaks
Towards the distant goal it seeks.

Straight to the guiding plane it flies
But takes the pilot by surprise.

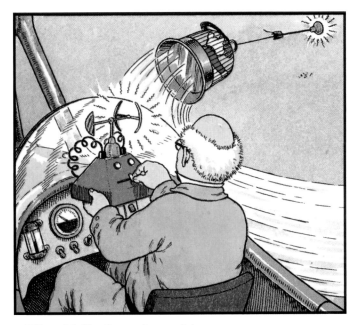

The old Professor keeps his nerve
And causes Rupert's cage to swerve.

The cage and arrow come in reach,
He quickly catches hold of each.

Down sweeps the birdcage behind the speeding boomerarrow. Rupert just hopes that Bingo's twine is good, strong stuff. Then the boomerarrow levels out and streaks towards a distant dot in the blue, a dot that grows until Rupert can see that it is the Professor's aircraft. His old friend must be controlling the boomerarrow from it. Now Rupert can see him clearly. His back is to the boomerarrow. Busy with the control device, does he know it is almost upon him? He turns.

His eyes widen in alarm. Can he get his machine out of the path of the boomerarrow in time? No! But he *can* change the boomerarrow's direction. He flicks a lever on the control device and boomerarrow and birdcage swerve at the last second. Then they make a wide circle, slowing until they stop beside the aircraft. The old man beams at Rupert as if nothing has happened. "I do hope you remembered to hold tight," he says.

RUPERT IS WELCOMED HOME

*"We don't want to upset the King.
We'll write and explain everything."*

*A welcome sight comes into view,
Bill, Bingo and his parents too.*

*Released at last, he leaves the cage.
It seems that he's been gone an age.*

*Happy now Rupert's home and free,
Everyone troops in for tea.*

With Rupert and cage safely aboard, the Professor's aircraft heads for Nutwood. On the way the friends agree that they'll write to the King of the Birds to apologise for almost hitting his Courier and upsetting his courtiers. "He knows me," Rupert says. "I'm quite sure he'll understand." At last the Professor's home appears and waiting there are Mr and Mrs Bear, Bingo, Bill and the Professor's servant who was sent to fetch them.

With a hacksaw the Professor's servant frees Rupert in no time at all. Rupert's parents, of course, are overjoyed to have him back safely. As they all make their way indoors, Bingo and the Professor ask how they can make up for their part in Rupert's misadventure. "Well, first, a promise – no more bow and arrow experiments," laughs Rupert. "Done!" cry the others. "Then tea and muffins, lots of them," Rupert adds. "I'm starving!" THE END.

RUPERT
and the
PEPPER-ROSE

A lost balloon leads Rupert to a garden where beautiful roses grow. From that moment, he finds himself mixed up in a mystery that makes people think he is playing pranks.

RUPERT GREETS HIS FRIENDS

"Why, that balloon looks bright and gay,"
Thinks Rupert, one fine summer's day.

Says Willie, "This balloon is new!
I'm sure the man has one for you."

"Yes, get one, Rupert – they're such fun,"
Calls Algy, "but you'll have to run!"

Soon from the hill-top Rupert sees
Balloons go bobbing past the trees.

One morning Rupert is strolling through Farmer Brown's grassy fields when he notices something bobbing along the top of the hedge. "It's a balloon," he thinks. "The path is over there. One of my pals must have it." Turning through the gate he discovers Willie. "Hello, Rupert," calls the little mouse. "Look at my fine balloon. It's a new kind and it's pulling upwards. If I don't keep a tight hold of the string it will float away into the sky!"

Willie tells Rupert that the wonderful balloons are being sold by a pedlar man over the hill. "They're jolly cheap and all our pals are buying them," he declares. "If you want one you'd better hurry before they are all gone." Thanking him, Rupert sets off and on the way he sees Algy and Reggie. "Are you wanting a balloon too?" says Algy. "You must hurry – the pedlar is moving on to the next village." So Rupert runs to the crest of the ridge. "There's the man," he murmurs.

RUPERT MAKES THE IMPS CROSS

But as he starts to hurry by,
He hears a little voice shout, "Hi!"

"Don't crush our bulbs, you clumsy thing!"
Exclaim the angry Imps of Spring.

"Next time be sure to look around,"
The Imp says, going underground.

So Rupert races off to buy
A new balloon that he can fly.

Rupert has hardly taken a dozen steps when a sharp cry pulls him up in his tracks. "Hi, what are you doing? Why can't you look where you're going?" A small angry voice calls him from the base of the tree and three of the Imps of Spring dash out and face him. "My, how you startled me!" Rupert quavers. "Have I done anything wrong?" "Wrong! Where are your eyes?" exclaims the first Imp. "Can't you see that our best late bulbs are just coming up? You're a big, careless, clumsy thing!" "I'm terribly sorry," says Rupert. "I was so anxious to find the balloon man that I didn't notice where I was running." Still grumbling, the Imps look around their bulbs and to their relief they find that he has not broken a single spike. "That's lucky for you," says the leader. "Be more careful next time. Now we must return to our work." They quickly disappear, while Rupert goes on his way and soon manages to overtake the man with the balloons.

25

RUPERT GLIDES OVER THE GRASS

Although it may not last for long,
The lifting gas is very strong.

Laughs Rupert, "Now if I hold tight
I'll sail along at quite a height!"

Across a ridge he takes a jump,
And lands again without a bump.

Then Rupert hears an angry shout,
And suddenly an Imp darts out.

To Rupert's delight the balloons are cheap, just as Willie said, and he quickly chooses one. "I've put some special lifting gas into them," says the man. "Its effect may not last for long, so have some fun while you can." "Yes, you're right," says the little bear as he moves happily away. "It pulls upwards. By holding onto it I can jump quite high! This is great. I must go and join the others!" And he makes his way back in a series of long leaps.

Rupert is so thrilled about his new game that he forgets everything else as he uses the balloon to help him jump over all the obstacles in his way. He has just cleared a low ridge when he is startled by another piercing cry, and an Imp of Spring darts at him. "What! You again?" screams the Imp. "You clumsy thing! Will you never learn to look where you're going?" Rupert turns in fright. "Goodness, I'm back at the bulb patch!" he gasps. "I'm sorry I didn't notice it when I landed."

RUPERT LOSES HIS FINE BALLOON

The little Imp upsets him so,
That Rupert suddenly lets go.

Sighs Rupert, "There goes my balloon!
Just fancy losing it so soon!"

He murmurs, "When I climb this slope,
I'll see my lost balloon, I hope."

The pedlar says, "A little breeze
Blew your balloon across those trees!"

More little angry Imps run out after their leader and examine their plants carefully. "You're lucky once more!" says one of them. "You've missed them again. There's no damage done, only I do wish you wouldn't keep frightening us." But Rupert is hardly listening. In his sudden agitation he has let go the string, and before he can grab it, the balloon has shot up and floated away. "Oh, what ever shall I do? I just can't lose it so soon!" he cries as he dashes over the fields in pursuit.

A light breeze wafts the balloon away just too fast for Rupert to keep pace with it. Trying to hold it in sight, he hurries up a long slope, but when he reaches the top it has disappeared. Breathless and disappointed, he pushes on. "Hello, there's the pedlar man again," he pants, running to the edge of the slope. "Please, my balloon's gone," he calls. "Have you seen it?" "Yes, that I have," says the man. "And you'll have a job to find it. I saw it dropping beyond that belt of trees . . ."

RUPERT FALLS OFF A HIGH WALL

Though Rupert's in the wood at last,
He cannot travel very fast.

"There's no way over this at all!"
Says Rupert, staring at the wall.

He finds a foothold soon enough,
Amongst the ivy, old and tough.

A crumbling stone makes Rupert lurch,
And sends him crashing from his perch.

Thanking the pedlar, Rupert forges ahead. "If the balloon has come down its lifting gas must have lost its power just as the man said it would," he mutters. He runs through the fringe of the wood, but soon he has to go more slowly, for the undergrowth becomes so thick that he has to struggle to make any headway. At length he reaches a clearing, only to find a worse obstacle in a huge wall that completely bars his way forward. The neglected ivy that is clinging to the wall is so old and strong that Rupert has no difficulty in climbing its tough branches to the top. "Oo, what a lovely garden down there," he thinks. "I believe I've seen it before, but I certainly didn't come this way. I wonder if I'd be allowed to get down and look for my balloon." At that moment a mossy stone on which he is leaning splits and crumbles, upsetting his balance. He cannot save himself and down he goes with a crash into a thick bush that breaks his fall.

RUPERT HAPPENS TO SEE MARY

Then as he rises from the ground,
He hears a kind of sneezing sound.

"It's Mary's garden, I can tell,"
Says Rupert, for he knows it well.

Gasps Mary, seeing him appear,
"How ever did you get in here?"

"Yes, your balloon dropped over there.
You'll never find it, little bear."

Picking himself up, Rupert finds that he is unhurt. "Whew, that was lucky," he murmurs, "but what do I do now?" As he pauses a strange sound reaches his ears. Then it comes again, and he realises that it is made by somebody sneezing. Moving on tip-toe towards the noise, he spies a little girl and as he approaches she sneezes again. "Now I know where I am!" he thinks. "That's Mary-Quite-Contrary, and this is her garden with the silver bells. I knew I'd been here before."

Mary-Quite-Contrary is very startled to see Rupert standing beside her. "How ever did you get in here?" she demands. "Please, I fell in – over your garden wall," says Rupert. "I'm very sorry, but I was trying to follow my balloon, and I don't know where it has gone." "Oh, but I think I do," Mary exclaims. "I saw a balloon floating over here, and it dropped gently into that thick clump of trees. I'm afraid you may never see it again in such a tangle of branches."

RUPERT HAS A FIT OF SNEEZING

She gives her friend, before he goes,
A very pretty single rose.

Then Mary says, "Now smell it, please."
The little bear begins to sneeze.

It smells of pepper, that they know,
But cannot think what makes it so.

"Ah, Daddy's handkerchief will hold
This rose you gave me," Mary's told.

Rupert is disappointed to think that he may have lost his new balloon so soon. "Ah well," he sighs, "it can't be helped. And now I must start for home again." Mary is quiet for a moment. "Before you go I want to show you a strange plant," she says. Moving to a bush of single roses, she picks a flower and asks him to smell it. Suspecting nothing, he sniffs it. All at once he gives a start and sneezes loudly again and again. When he has recovered Rupert gazes at the rose.

"That was a fine trick to play on anybody!" he gasps. "What sort of flower is this?" "I only wish I knew," laughs Mary. "I hoped you could help me find out. I was caught by it just before you came in. I expect you heard me sneezing too." "I'd love to try to help you," says Rupert eagerly. "It smells of pepper. May I take it and ask my friends? It's lucky I have one of Daddy's handkerchiefs. I can wrap it up so that I don't sneeze." "Why yes, that's a good idea," says Mary.

RUPERT IS GUIDED TO THE BOAT

The little bear hears Mary say,
"You'd better go the other way."

"But here's the end of your grass track,"
Sighs Rupert, "so we must turn back."

Then Rupert peers in great surprise,
"Why, here's a little boat!" he cries.

So Rupert steps into the boat,
And down the stream he starts to float.

Once the strange flower is safely folded in the handkerchief, Rupert sighs and walks back to the wall. "Now I suppose I've got the job of climbing it again," he murmurs. "Hi! Where are you going?" Mary calls. "Nobody is supposed to go up there! Let me show you a better way." She take him along a track through very high grass until they reach a little stream. "But surely this doesn't lead anywhere at all!" exclaims Rupert. Mary-Quite-Contrary smiles to see Rupert's puzzled expression.

"You're quite right," she answers. "The path stops here. But I didn't say you were going out of my garden by a path, did I?" Just beyond some bushes she begins to untie a cord that is wound round a post. "I say, what a topping little boat!" cries Rupert. "Yes, it's mine. You may get in if you like," says Mary. She holds the boat steady until the little bear has clambered in, and a moment later he finds himself drifting gently down the stream.

RUPERT FLOATS ALONG A TUNNEL

The little bear exclaims, "Oh, my!
This archway isn't very high!"

Although the tunnel's rather low,
Straight through it Rupert Bear must go.

"Ah, now I'm out again!" says he,
And grabs an overhanging tree.

Then back the boat begins to glide,
And soon it disappears inside.

Rupert is still mystified. "Do you mean that I have to go out this way?" he asks. "If so, how can I send the boat back to you?" "Can't you see that I am still holding it by the cord?" says Mary. "It won't get away from me." Drifting into the current, Rupert finds himself heading again for the great wall. "Why, there's a tunnel! How exciting!" he breathes. He hears the cheerful voice of Mary bidding him goodbye and then he enters the gloom.

After a while he emerges at the far end and finds that the little stream is overhung by a thick wood. Grabbing a branch he hauls himself on to the bank. "Now I'd better shout to let Mary know I'm safe, and she can pull her boat home." But as he turns round he sees that the small craft is already disappearing back into the darkness, drawn along by the cord. "My, what a whopping big wall," Rupert mutters. "No wonder it is such a difficult garden for anyone to get into."

RUPERT ANNOYS THE DWARF

"The old Professor lives up there,
I'll visit him!" says Rupert Bear.

Calls Rupert, "Fancy meeting you!
I'm going to the castle, too!"

"Well, what's so strange about this rose?"
Demands the dwarf – but soon he knows!

"So that's the sort of trick you play!"
The dwarf exclaims. "Now run away!"

When he has struggled out of the wood, Rupert gazes round to get his bearings. "I wonder who would know most about this queer rose," he thinks. " The old Professor's the cleverest person I know, and – yes – I can see his house over there. I'll ask him." Hurrying into the hollow, he climbs the slope opposite. Long before he reaches the house, he meets the Professor's dwarf servant. "Hello, is your master in?" he calls, and snatches the handkerchief from the rose. "I want to show him this flower." The dwarf servant takes the rose and gazes at it. "Hm! It seems a very ordinary colour," he says. "What's strange about it?" He sniffs casually and then he knows. When his tremendous fit of sneezing is over he glares at Rupert. "Oh, so that was what you were going to do to my master, was it?" he shouts. "You mischievous little creature. Be off with you!" He seems so angry that Rupert seizes the rose and does not wait to explain.

"It's no use trying to explain,"
Sighs Rupert, setting off again.

"I'm coming, Rupert," Rastus calls,
And through the wooden bars he crawls.

The country mouse says, "Let me see!
Do show your special rose to me!"

"A-tchoo!" gasps Rastus Mouse, "a-tchoo!
That was a silly thing to do!"

Before he has gone far Rupert pauses. "I wish I could be allowed to take this flower to the Professor himself," he thinks. "I'm sure he would be interested. He may never have seen one like it before." But the dwarf is still annoyed and is watching him sternly, so he continues on his way. "I wonder who else there is who would know about roses," he mutters. He does not notice that one of his pals, Rastus the Country Mouse, is watching him inquisitively.

After wriggling through the fence, Rastus calls to Rupert. "Hi! Where are you going? Who was that shouting at you just now? What are you carrying in that handkerchief?" The little bear gazes at him with a smile, then he tells about the queer rose from the garden of Mary-Quite-Contrary. "I'm from the country. I know all about flowers. Show it to me," says Rastus. Next moment he is wishing that he had not held it so close to his nose.

34

RUPERT JUST MISSES SOME SHOOTS

"You caught me then, without a doubt,"
Laughs Rastus, "but I'll pay you out!"

As Rupert dodges round and round,
He hears a shrill and angry sound.

The leading Imp cries, "Your big boots
Will spoil our pretty little shoots."

Says Rupert, "I am glad we've met,
You haven't seen this strange rose yet."

When he has finished sneezing and has wiped the tears out of his eyes Rastus grins. "Fancy me being caught by a trick like that!" he squeaks. "Just you wait. I'll pay you out, young Rupert!" He waves his stick and pretends to be fierce, while Rupert, who has meanwhile picked up the rose, laughs and runs away. Round and round they go, dodging between trees and bushes until a now familiar voice pulls them up suddenly and puts a stop to their capers.

At the sight of the tiny strangers Rastus runs away in fright, but Rupert pauses in anxiety and faces the Imps of Spring. "It really is too bad!" cries the leading Imp. "I *told* you to keep away from our special bulb patch and this is the third time today you've come dashing across it!" All at once Rupert has an idea. "I'm awfully sorry," he says, "but please don't be angry. I think you're just the people to tell me what this is." And hopefully he shows them the pepper-rose.

The pepper scent is very strong
And makes the Imp sneeze loud and long.

Next moment Rupert Bear is seized,
Those Imps of Spring are so displeased!

The leader frowns, "We never meant
A rose to have this horrid scent."

"We'll help, for something must be done,"
Agree the Imps, and off they run.

The pepper-rose has just the same effect on the leading Imp as on everyone else and he is taken at once with a violent fit of sneezing. The other Imps are indignant at what they think is a trick and they seize Rupert and pull him down, but the leader stops them. "Let him alone," he orders. "Spring flowers are our affair, but this is none of our doing. Tell me, little bear, where did you find it? Are there more of them? This matter is important to us."

Rupert gets up with relief. "Please, the rose belongs to Mary-Quite-Contrary," he says. "There's a bush covered with them in her garden. She can't understand them and I'm trying to find somebody who does. Can you help me?" "But we *must* help," says the leading Imp. "That's our job. I never sent Mary a flower like this. Roses should not smell of pepper! Come, let us look at our records." Telling Rupert to follow, the Imps of Spring all race away across a stretch of sloping ground.

RUPERT CRAWLS UNDERGROUND

Then one cries, "Aren't you coming too?
This hole is big enough for you."

"Do hurry up," the small folk say,
And run ahead to show the way.

"We'll find the answer here, perhaps,"
The Imps say, looking at some maps.

Then Rupert follows to the store
Until they reach a little door.

Soon the tiny people reach a very big tree and disappear down a dark hollow at its base, but Rupert pauses and peeps in. Before long one of the Imps returns and beckons. "Aren't you coming?" he demands impatiently. "Am I allowed to?" asks Rupert nervously. "Of course," cries the other. "Our leader chose this way because it's big enough for you." So Rupert squeezes between the roots, until he is in a long rough passage in the earth.

When Rupert and his tiny friend rejoin the others they find the leader busily scanning one of a row of maps. "H'm, yes, there's Mary's garden, right over our stores," he murmurs. "Now we know where to look for the cause of the trouble." He writes instructions on a piece of paper and sends one of the Imps off with it. "May I go with him?" Rupert asks. The leader says he may, so the little bear hurries through a small doorway and down another tunnel where the Imps keep their stores.

RUPERT'S MYSTERY IS SOLVED

The Imp remarks, "Now we are here,
I don't know what to do, I fear."

"Ah, look! The rose-bush roots have got
Inside our great big pepper-pot!"

They hurry out again to tell
How roses get a sneezing smell.

"We thought that you were up to pranks,
But now you've earned our grateful thanks."

At length the Imp pauses and looks puzzled. "Here we are, Rupert, right under the garden of Mary-Quite-Contrary," he says. "I wonder what I'm supposed to look for." Suddenly he starts forward. "Do you see what I see?" he gasps. "Someone has left the top of the pepper-pot off and, look, there are some roots going right into it. Those must be the roots of the bush that grows the pepper-roses. Quick, we must let the others know about this!"

The Imp loses no time in telling the others about what he has discovered. "What," cries the leader. "So it really *is* a pepper-rose! One of us must have been very careless to leave the top off the pepper-pot. It's not often we make mistakes like that. It must never happen again. Our roses must smell like roses, not like pepper!" Then he leads Rupert out. "You have done us a good turn, little bear," he smiles. "I hope we may do one for you some day to repay you for your help."

"If we can find your lost balloon,"
The Imp says, "you will have it soon."

The little bear runs home at last,
For now the fuss is solved and past.

Though Mummy's warned she sniffs the rose,
And gets the pepper in her nose.

The red balloon, still with its string,
Comes back – sent by the Imps of Spring!

Before Rupert has gone far the Imp appears again. "Here is your pepper-rose," he says. "I expect you'll like to keep it. We will get some for ourselves from Mary's garden." "Oh, if you're going there I wish you'd look for my beautiful balloon," Rupert exclaims, and he tells the other of his adventure. "Of course we will!" cries the Imp. "If your balloon is there we'll bring it back to you! Leave it to us, little bear." And, feeling much happier, Rupert scampers home.

He tells his Mummy all about his adventure and, although she has been warned, she sniffs at the rose! "I must write and tell Mary-Quite-Contrary what has made her roses smell of pepper!" Rupert laughs, when his Mummy stops sneezing. "She will have a surprise." Then he gives a gasp of delight. "Look, look, here is my beautiful balloon floating in at the window! Those Imps of Spring have found it and brought it back. How fast they work! Now everything is right again!" THE END.

RUPERT and

RUPERT IS OFF TO THE SEASIDE

"I'll soon see Sandy Bay again!"
Thinks Rupert, gazing from the train.

He hears a gruff voice, "In you go!
Your tickets aren't first class, you know!"

The summer holiday is here at last. After the exciting bustle of getting ready, Mr and Mrs Bear are taking Rupert on the train to Sandy Bay. Kneeling by the window, Rupert gazes at the passing countryside and listens to the clicking of the wheels. All at once he is startled to hear a gruff voice: "In you go. And mind you behave yourselves!" The little bear swings round, and who should he see but Freddy and Ferdy Fox being

thrust into the compartment by an angry ticket inspector. "Why, what are they doing on this train?" thinks Rupert. "I caught these young imps in a first-class compartment with second-class tickets," says the man. "They tried to hide from me under the seats, but I was too quick for them." "Oh please, we weren't really to blame," whimpers Freddy. "We were late getting to the station. The train was already in."

the SECRET SHELL

At the start of his seaside holiday, Rupert visits Captain Barnacle, who shows him a game to play using the Sea Sprite figurehead which stands beside his shack. And how important that very game proves to be when later Rupert meets some real Sea Sprites.

RUPERT TRAVELS WITH TWO FOXES

Says the inspector, "Watch them, please!"
And startled, Mr Bear agrees.

"Our Auntie lives at Sandy Bay,
She's meeting us," the foxes say.

"Yes," says Ferdy. "We had to jump in quickly. We didn't look to see which class it was." "That's no excuse," mutters the inspector. "You know very well this is a corridor train. You could easily have walked along to a second-class compartment." The foxes are lost for words. "I see your tickets are for Sandy Bay," remarks the inspector. "Yes, that is where our Auntie Vixen lives," mumbles Freddy. "We are going to spend a holiday with her."

"Then stay here for the rest of the journey," says the inspector. "I'll have no more nonsense." He turns to Mr Bear. "Would you see them safely to Sandy Bay, sir?" Mr Bear agrees, and quietly tells the mischievous foxes to behave themselves. "So you are off to Sandy Bay too," says Rupert. "It's odd that we're going to the same place. I wonder what adventures we shall have during our holiday."

41

RUPERT GAZES AT THE WATER

"I'll see you later – on the beach!"
Calls Rupert, with a wave to each.

"Explore the sands now, if you wish,
But don't touch any jellyfish!"

Grins Ferdy, "Won't you change your mind?
The pier's a nicer place, you'll find!"

"The tide is in, that's what they mean,"
Breathes Rupert, gazing at the scene.

At last the train arrives at Sandy Bay station. The doors open, and everyone streams out. The foxes' Auntie Vixen is waiting at the barrier, and Mrs Bear pauses for a chat with her. "Cheerio for now!" calls Rupert, when they go their separate ways. "I'll see you later – on the beach!" The Bears are soon settled in their holiday home. "May I go out while you are unpacking, Mummy?" asks Rupert. "Of course," says Mrs Bear. Reaching the sea-front Rupert spies the foxes.

"Hi!" he calls. "Are you coming on the sands?" "No, we'd rather go on the pier first," grins Freddy. The brothers stroll away, and, feeling rather puzzled, Rupert makes for the seawall. Peering over the side he sees deep water swirling below him. "So that's why they wouldn't come," he mutters. "It's high tide, and there's no sand to play on!" Fanned by little gusts of salty spray, he stares out to sea and wonders how to pass the time until the tide goes out.

RUPERT SPENDS A HAPPY TIME

"Old Captain Barnacle lives here,
I'll visit him, his shack's quite near."

The captain's working on a boat,
He smiles, "My models really float."

"That figurehead is very old,
Though new to this place," Rupert's told.

"It's from a grand old ship of mine,
The 'Sea Sprite' – don't you think it's fine?"

"I'll visit Captain Barnacle," decides Rupert. Leaving the sea-front he clambers up to the old man's cliff-top shack. Tapping gently on the door, he goes in and finds his friend busy carving a model of a boat. The captain greets him heartily. "So you can't go on the beach, eh? You'd better keep me company until low tide!" he chuckles. For some time the little bear enjoys watching him at work. Then, just as Rupert is growing fidgety, the captain lays down his work.

"I've something new – but very old – that'll make time fly for you!" he says. "I'll show you." "Oo, what is it? Where is it?" asks Rupert. Getting up, the captain points through a window. "It's a figurehead from a grand old ship of mine called the Sea Sprite. But come and take a closer look." Rupert scampers outside, followed by his friend. "My, doesn't it look lifelike! And what a lovely shell it's holding!" gasps the little bear. "It's very old just as you said. But how can it make time fly?"

RUPERT LEARNS HOW TO PLAY

Then Rupert's taught a lovely game!
Each throws in turn, with careful aim.

"You've scored the most, I do declare!
And now the tide's out, little bear."

To Rupert's joy, he finds a pool
By rocks surrounded, deep and cool.

He scoops a shell out, "My, how strange!
It's like . . ." Then the foxes come in range.

Captain Barnacle takes a ball from his pocket, then, with careful aim, he tosses it and – plop! – it drops straight into the Sea Sprite's shell. "Shiver my timbers!" cries the captain. "For once I've scored first try. Your shot, Rupert!" They throw in turn, until Rupert has scored more than the captain. "I give in," chuckles the old sailor. "You've won!" "The Sea Sprite did make time fly," says Rupert. "It was good fun." Returning indoors, Captain Barnacle checks his chart.

"The tide is out now," he says. So Rupert says goodbye to his old friend. Then he hurries down to the seashore and to his delight finds a deep pool. "I can see lots of tiny fishes flashing about," he murmurs. "And – oh! – there's something else." Rupert feels among the seaweed and suddenly finds himself clasping a large shell. "How strange!" he breathes. "It's exactly like . . ." At that moment he notices the Fox brothers looking for shrimps. "What have you found?" they call.

RUPERT LETS FERDY FOX LISTEN

*"A voice is whispering! Oh, my!
'Go to that cave,' I heard it sigh."*

*"I'll show the captain! Give it back!
It's like that carved shell by his shack!"*

*"That voice told me just where to go!
So round that headland we shall row!"*

*As Rupert Bear turns sadly round,
He hears a tiny sobbing sound.*

"That's a fine shell, Rupert," remarks Ferdy. "Have you heard the sea in it?" "Not yet," says Rupert. "I'll let you try it first." He hands the shell to Ferdy, who holds it to his ear and listens intently. Suddenly his grin fades, and he frowns. "A voice whispered to me!" he breathes. "It told me to go to a cave on the far side of the headland!" "A voice? Are you sure?" says Rupert. "I'd like to hear it too." To his dismay Ferdy clutches the shell tightly and backs away.

"The voice spoke to *me!*" he insists. "I'm keeping this shell!" "You can't!" cries Rupert anxiously. "I must show it to Captain Barnacle. It's exactly like the shell on his ship's figurehead. Now please give me the shell!" "Not likely! Who cares about an old figurehead!" retorts Ferdy. "We mean to find out why the magic voice told us to go there!" With that, the Fox brothers take to their heels. "It's no use, they won't give it back," sighs the little bear, turning sadly away along the seashore.

RUPERT BELIEVES HE CAN HELP

"I'm Ripple! Yes, a Sprite, indeed!
But I can't find the shell I need."

The Sea Sprite sobs, "This shell can speak,
And guide me to the king I seek."

"I'm sure I found that shell just now!
Wait here, I'll get it back somehow!"

"Oh dear, where have those foxes gone?"
Says Rupert, roaming on and on.

Reaching a heap of rocks, Rupert is astonished to see a small figure searching through some seaweed. "Why, you're a real Sea Sprite!" he gasps. "Yes, I'm Ripple," sighs the Sprite. "I've travelled from a far land to seek my king." Then, covering his face with his hands, Ripple sobs bitterly. "What ever is wrong?" asks Rupert. "I'm looking for a secret shell," murmurs the Sprite. "A voice inside it can tell me the way to the Sprite King's palace. And unless I show the shell, I shall not be allowed in. Alas, I cannot find it here." "Sit down, and tell me what the secret shell looks like," says Rupert. The Sprite does so, and Rupert nods. "That's the very shell I found!" he exclaims. "And – yes! – a voice told Ferdy to . . ." "Oh, have you got it?" asks Ripple hopefully. "Not now, but I know who has! I'll soon get it back!" cries Rupert. "Just wait here for me." The little bear races along the sands in search of Ferdy and Freddy, but they are nowhere to be seen.

RUPERT BORROWS THE CARVING

"They went to find a boat – that's right!
No wonder they are out of sight!"

"The carved shell!" Rupert starts to run,
"Could it replace the other one?"

He puffs, "Oh, Captain, would you lend
Your carved shell to my Sea Sprite friend?"

"The secret shell's a pass, no less,
That's why the Sprite was in distress."

After searching the beach, Rupert climbs some steps to get a better view, but he still cannot trace the foxes. "I'm too late," he murmurs. "And the secret shell is with them! How ever can I tell the Sprite?" Rupert's thoughts turn to Captain Barnacle. Suddenly he has an idea, and, swinging round, he races along the sea-front. "The carved shell!" he breathes. "It's exactly like the real one! Perhaps the captain will let me borrow it if I tell him about the Sprite." On arriving at the shack,

Rupert finds his old friend working on some nets. "Please," puffs the little bear. "May I borrow your Sea Sprite's shell? It's needed by a real Sea Sprite!" "A *real* one?" gasps the captain. "But what's all this about?" As soon as Rupert has told his story, Captain Barnacle hurries with him to the figurehead. "It's a poor world if one Sea Sprite can't help another!" he chuckles, as he lifts out the carved shell and gives it to Rupert. "There you are. Take it for your little friend."

RUPERT DARTS ALONG THE SHORE

"Ah, thank you! That will do instead!
Now, tell me what that shell-voice said!"

"I'll find that cave! But, little bear,
Your friends are in great danger there!"

"I'll have to warn them! There they are!"
Frowns Rupert. "They're all right so far."

"I must keep up at any cost,
If I lose sight of them, they're lost!"

Rupert thanks Captain Barnacle, then carries the shell to where the Sprite is still waiting. "It's only a carved one," says Rupert, and he explains what has happened. "No one at the palace will guess," replies the Sprite, "but it can't guide me there." Rupert tells him the message that Ferdy heard in the real shell. "It's lucky you remembered!" cries Ripple happily. "I'll soon find that cave. But those foxes will be in great danger if they go there!" The little bear starts forward in alarm.

"What do you mean about the foxes being in danger?" he calls. But Ripple has already disappeared among the rocks. "Oh dear," sighs Rupert. "It's all so mysterious." Just then he spies a boat out in the bay. "It's Ferdy and Freddy!" he gasps. "I'm sure of it!" Rupert dashes along the shore, trying to draw level with the boat. "I simply must see where they go," he mutters. "I need the secret shell! Besides, I ought to warn them not to go near the cave."

RUPERT CLAMBERS OVER ROCKS

He stops, dismayed! It looks as if
His way is blocked by that gaunt cliff.

He starts to climb, with careful grip,
"I'll be all right if I don't slip!"

"They're landing now, I'm just in time!"
Gasps Rupert, breathless from his climb.

Then crowds of angry Sprites stream out,
Their screeching drowns his warning shout!

Rupert manages to keep the foxes' boat in sight until he finds his way cut off by a cliff which juts into the sea. The little bear is dismayed, but he does not hesitate for long. "I can just about get round," he says as he clambers over the jagged rocks. "Perhaps it's not far to the next bay." He soon finds himself climbing higher and higher. A seagull gives its lonely cry, then all is silent. "I don't like the look of this," mutters Rupert, glancing at the swirling water below. "I hope I don't slip." Rupert is relieved when he reaches a wide ledge. He scrambles down just in time to see Ferdy and Freddy tying up their boat. The brothers step ashore and make straight for a huge open shell which is standing near by. "They shouldn't have come here. I must warn them about the danger!" gasps the little bear, creeping forward. But he is too late. Angry Sprites are already streaming from the cave. Rupert bobs down in alarm, but the foxes have not yet noticed.

RUPERT PLEADS WITH A SPRITE

They seize the brothers, bind them well,
And push them to their giant shell.

The last Sprite gives an angry cry:
"Look, here's a third! He's come to spy!"

"Keep back! How dare you interfere!
They must be punished, do you hear?"

"Now, stranger, just explain yourself,
You're trespassing upon this shelf!"

The little bear tries to warn the foxes. "Look out!" he cries. "Run for the boat!" The brothers glance up, but by then the Sprites have surrounded them. "Who are you?" they screech. "How dare you pry into our secrets?" And before Rupert can do anything Freddy and Ferdy are bound with seaweed cords. Then they are pushed roughly towards the great shell. Suddenly one of their captors rounds furiously on Rupert. "Here's another intruder!" he shrieks.

"We'll come back and deal with him later!" Rupert rushes forwards to try to save the foxes, but the Sprites will not listen to him. They drag him back, and hustle Freddy and Ferdy into the shell. The foxes squeal for help, but worse is to follow. No sooner are they in the shell than one of the Sprites closes the top and imprisons the unhappy brothers. "Please set them free!" begs Rupert. "They didn't mean any harm." But the Sprites shake their heads firmly and refuse to let him pass.

He pleads again, in great alarm,
"Please let them out! They meant no harm."

"I'm here!" cries Ripple. "Come with me,
Our king's the one whom you must see."

"We'll play your new game. Please begin.
I'll free those foxes if you win!"

With that the king stands up and calls,
A courtier brings some seaweed balls.

Rupert turns in despair to another Sprite. "Please, the foxes only meant to obey the secret shell," he cries. "I came to warn them. Oh, please let them out!" "That I cannot do," snaps the other. "They are trespassers . . ." He breaks off as a voice exclaims: "The little bear is my friend!" "Why, Ripple! It's you!" cries Rupert joyfully. The friendly Sprite darts forward, hugging the carved shell. "Take this shell, and come with me!" he cries. "You must make your request to our monarch." Before long the little bear stands in front of the Sprite King. In a faltering voice, Rupert pleads for the foxes, but the king refuses to free them. Luckily the little bear suddenly thinks of a plan. "Then let me try to win their freedom, your Majesty," he implores. "Let me challenge your Sprites to a match!" He describes Captain Barnacle's game, and the king begins to smile. "I wish to see this game," he commands. And he sends for a tray of seaweed balls.

RUPERT HAS THE BEST SCORE

"This game's an easy one to learn,"
Rupert explains. "Each takes a turn."

The match begins, the Sprites throw first,
Breathes Rupert, "This part is the worst."

The Sprites score four, then Rupert throws,
He must *get five to win, he knows.*

To free his chums, he tries his best,
"I've won!" he cries. "I've passed your test!"

"We shall also need three big shells," Rupert says, as the king leads him outside. The Sprites search for the largest shells they can find, and meanwhile Rupert tells the king how the game should be played. "It sounds difficult," says the monarch. "And if you win the foxes shall go free." He gives a signal and the game begins. Rupert watches anxiously. The Sprites throw first, but their aim is poor, and when the last ball is thrown their score stands at four. Then it is Rupert's turn,

and he gets ready to beat the Sprites' score. "I won when I played this game for fun," he murmurs. "Now I must win the foxes' freedom!" He takes aim, but the slippery seaweed balls are not easy to throw, and several of his shots miss the shells. When he pauses to count, he has scored four. "One more to win!" he breathes. "Oh, my! This is the last ball!" Rupert tries his very best, and to his delight the ball drops neatly into a shell. "I've won!" he cries.

RUPERT'S REQUEST IS GRANTED

"Well done!" the little king commends,
"You've earned a pardon for your friends."

"Release the captives, and unbind
Their seaweed cords! I've changed my mind!"

Rupert explains about the game,
Then hears the monarch call his name.

"Once home, a message you shall hear,
Just put the carved shell to your ear."

The little monarch smiles at Rupert. "Well done!" he exclaims. "Your skill shall be rewarded." Attended by his chief courtier, he leads Rupert and Ripple along a ledge to a rocky platform. "What is your Majesty's pleasure?" cry the Sprites who are guarding the brothers. "Open the shell and release the captives!" commands the king. "This little bear has won their freedom!" The guards hurry to obey, and presently Rupert glimpses the foxes as the shell slowly opens. The brothers are quickly unbound and helped from the shell. "How miserable they look," thinks Rupert. When they hear that Rupert has won their freedom, Ferdy and Freddy burst into tears. "W-we thought we'd never get out," sobs Ferdy. The king asks for Captain Barnacle's carved shell and, raising his hands above it, he whispers some strange words. "Now take the shell, little bear," he commands. "When you reach home, hold it to your ear and you will hear a message!"

"I have no words for you, except –
Give back the secret shell you kept!"

"You're quite safe now, don't shiver so!"
Smiles Rupert, as he helps to row.

"Return the boat! You mustn't wait,
They'll charge you extra if you're late!"

Then Rupert sets off at a run,
To tell the captain all he's done.

Feeling very thrilled, Rupert takes the carved shell and murmurs, "Thank you!" Then Ripple helps him into the boat and rather wistfully says goodbye. The king turns sternly to the Fox brothers. "Give back our secret shell!" he commands. "Then hurry hence – never to come here again!" The dismal pair obey and are only too glad to tumble into the boat and push away from the ledge. Rupert takes one of the oars and helps Freddy to row. "You're safe now," smiles the little bear.

Rupert and Freddy row round the headland, then they pull in so that Rupert can get ashore, "I must return Captain Barnacle's shell," he says. "And we must take back the boat," replies Freddy. "My! I don't want another adventure like that one!" Rupert clambers up the cliff steps to find Captain Barnacle. "Here's your shell!" cries the little bear. "And what do you think? There's magic in it! The Sprite King . . ." "Whoa! Not so fast!" interrupts the captain.

RUPERT CATCHES THE MESSAGE

The story leaves his friend spellbound,
He cries, "Quick, listen for a sound!"

Gasps Rupert, "Why, it's telling me
To look for something by the sea!"

The little bear, when all is still,
Returns the carved shell, with a thrill.

"I'm glad the Sea Sprite's shell is back,"
He says, while they enjoy a snack.

Captain Barnacle sits quietly while the little bear gasps out his story. When Rupert has finished the old sailor jumps to his feet. "Let's see what happens," he cries. "Put the shell to your ear, Rupert!" Excitedly the little bear obeys. At first he hears only the rushing of waves, then the sound changes to strange echoing words, "Sh-ssh!" whispers the voice. "At the next low tide, go down to the shore! You will find something there. Sh-ssh!" Then all is quiet. "Well?" says the captain.

"What did you hear?" He is thrilled when Rupert tells him about the whispered message. "It's some time to the next low tide," he says. "We'll have something to eat while we wait." First they go to the figurehead and, lifted by the captain, Rupert places the shell in the Sea Sprite's hands. Then they return to the shack, and as soon as they are indoors Captain Barnacle sets the table. "The magic's gone now, but I'm glad your Sea Sprite has the shell back," smiles Rupert.

RUPERT'S FRIEND SPIES A FISH

"Low tide is not for some time yet,
Let's listen to my wireless set!"

The captain hurries out at last,
"Ah! Something's moving very fast!"

A fish leaps up, how large it seems!
And in its mouth a necklace gleams!

Now Rupert waits to hear no more,
He dashes down to search the shore.

After their meal, Rupert and Captain Barnacle pass the time by listening-in on an old-fashioned radio set. At last the captain says, "It's time we were on the look-out." Picking up his telescope he goes to the cliff-top, and Rupert follows him. "Isn't it exciting!" says the little bear. "I wonder what we shall find." The captain peers out to sea through his glass, while Rupert scans the shore. "Why, fancy that!" exclaims the old man suddenly. A large fish leaps from the water again and in its mouth is something that looks like a necklace. "He's coming nearer!" cries the old sailor. "There! He's tossed it ashore. And now he's disappeared!" Filled with excitement, Rupert rushes down the cliff steps and leaps on to the sand. "Steady," calls the captain, following as quickly as he can. But Rupert is already searching, and suddenly he shouts: "There's something over here. Can't you see it glinting? I must get it before the waves wash it out to sea!"

RUPERT PICKS UP A NECKLACE

Upon the sands a necklace glints,
With lovely deep-pink sunset tints.

"That's beautiful!" The captain stares,
"It's made of coral," he declares.

"That kind of coral's very rare!
Well, I won't keep you, little bear."

"Whatever will my Mummy say?"
Breathes Rupert, on his homeward way.

The little bear walks towards the glittering object, which lies near the water's edge. Then he stoops and picks up the most beautiful necklace he has ever seen. Its deep-pink beads glow like a sunset. "Oo, how pretty it is!" he breathes, holding up the necklace to show Captain Barnacle. "It's made of coral!" exclaims the old sailor. "I've seen some on my voyages, but none as lovely as this! It grows under the sea, near hot, sunny lands. I'd no idea that the Sea Sprites travelled to such far-off places!" "I'll give the necklace to Mummy," says Rupert. "Then she's very lucky," smiles Captain Barnacle. "This is a rare kind of coral. Well, I won't keep you." Saying goodbye, the old captain starts to climb the cliff steps. Rupert waves cheerily, then, carrying the necklace, he runs along the sands. Soon he is mounting the slope to the sea-front, and he slows down a little to get his breath back. "The necklace must be a gift from the Sprite King," he thinks.

RUPERT BRINGS MUMMY A GIFT

"That boat-trip cost us all we had,
That's why we're feeling very sad."

"Cheer up! I know a grand new game!
We'll have a good time, just the same!"

Cries Rupert, "I want you to keep
This coral necklace from the deep."

Smiles Mummy, "It's a gorgeous one!"
Then Rupert tells her all he's done.

When he steps on to the promenade, Rupert is surprised to find Ferdy and Freddy leaning against the wall, looking very glum. "Hello again!" he calls. "What's the matter?" "We had to pay extra for keeping the boat out so long," says Ferdy gloomily. "We've no pocket-money left." "Never mind," says Rupert. "We can have fun on the beach tomorrow without any money." The brothers brighten. "You always think of jolly games," they smile. "See you tomorrow then," says the little bear. "I must rush home now. I'm awfully late!" Racing back, Rupert meets Mr and Mrs Bear. "Look! Here's a present for you, Mummy!" he cries, showing the necklace. "It's real coral!" gasps Daddy. They hurry indoors, and Mrs Bear tries on her present. "It's lovely!" she smiles. "You usually find some shells – but I didn't expect a necklace!" "Well, it was a special shell that started my adventure with the Sea Sprites," says Rupert. "I'll tell you about it!" THE END.

RUPERT
and the
Sundial

John Harrold.

RUPERT FEELS HOT

A long hot summer pleases some,
But Rupert's dad wants rain to come . . .

Mrs Bear says, "Don't be dismayed!
I'll make us all some lemonade . . ."

Bill Badger's mother stops to say,
"Another lovely sunny day . . ."

"We're out of lemons, I'm afraid!"
Says Mr Chimp. "Try orangeade!"

It has been a long, hot summer in Nutwood, with the sun blazing down every day . . . "This can't go on much longer!" complains Mr Bear. "If it doesn't rain soon the garden will be ruined! The lawn looks parched, the roses are over and everything else is wilting." "It is rather hot!" agrees Mrs Bear. "I think we could all do with a nice cool drink! How about some lemonade?" "Yes, please!" says Rupert. "Coming up!" smiles Mrs Bear. "I'll just go and buy some lemons . . ."

Rupert decides to go with his mother to the shops. On the way there, the pair meet Bill and Mrs Badger. "Hello!" she smiles. "Isn't this heat-wave lovely? I can't remember when it last rained!" "Me neither!" laughs Mrs Bear. When they reach the village shop, Rupert and his mother see that they are not the only ones to think of making lemonade . . . "Sold out of lemons, I'm afraid!" says Mr Chimp. "These little oranges are all I'll have now, until next week's delivery."

RUPERT MEETS PODGY PIG

"I'll go this way, if you don't mind,
There might be some pals I can find . . ."

"There's Podgy Pig! He's playing catch –
Perhaps he'd like a football match?"

"Hello!" calls Podgy. "Look at me!
I've learnt to juggle! Come and see . . ."

"It's fun with fruit!" says Podgy. "You
Can juggle some, then eat it too!"

As Mrs Bear returns with a bag of oranges, Rupert decides to take a longer path across the common to see if he can spot any of his chums. "See you later!" calls his mother. "Don't get too hot in the sun!" Rupert hasn't gone far when he spots his pal, Podgy, playing with an orange ball. "I wonder what he's up to?" he thinks. "Now it's a yellow ball he's got . . ." Full of curiosity, Rupert hurries across the common towards his chum, who seems to be completely engrossed . . .

As Rupert gets nearer, he sees that Podgy is busy juggling . . . "Those aren't balls!" he gasps. "They're oranges and lemons!" "Hello!" smiles Podgy. "You didn't know I could do this, did you?" "No!" admits Rupert. "Neither did I!" laughs his chum. "I had to practise for ages before I got it right!" Podgy stops juggling and starts to peel one of the enormous oranges. "Time for another snack!" he declares. "They're really delicious. Try a piece and see for yourself . . ."

RUPERT IS GIVEN AN ORANGE

"Delicious!" Rupert cries. "But all
The oranges we saw were small . . . "

"Not these!" laughs Podgy gleefully.
"I picked them myself – from the tree!"

"Have one!" says Podgy. "I know where
To find so much, I've fruit to spare!"

"How odd!" thinks Rupert. "Is it true?
I wonder where this orange grew?

"You're right!" says Rupert as he bites into the orange. "It's juicier than the ones we normally get . . ." "Bigger too!" nods Podgy. "I could only fit six in my basket!" "Wherever did they come from?" asks Rupert. "Mr Chimp's sold out!" "I know!" chuckles Podgy. "But these aren't from a shop. I picked them myself, straight from the tree . . ." "Picked them?" marvels Rupert. "Where?" "That would be telling!" smiles Podgy. "If everyone finds out, they'll all disappear!"

No matter how much Rupert asks him, Podgy refuses to say another word about where he found the oranges. "You can have one from my basket to take home," he declares. "But the tree's a secret. Only I know where it is – and that's how it's going to stay!" Rupert stares at the orange as Podgy marches away. "I can't believe it grew in Nutwood!" he gasps. "Perhaps Podgy got them from Tigerlily? Or perhaps he went for a ride in PongPing's lift? I wonder if oranges grow in China?"

RUPERT SEES AN OLD PICTURE

"Look, Dad!" cries Rupert. "Do you know
Where oranges like this one grow?"

"In Nutwood?" murmurs Mr Bear.
"The weather's too cold for them here."

"You can grow oranges on trees
In special glasshouses – like these . . ."

"That house is one I recognise –
It's Nutwood Manor!" Rupert cries.

When Rupert gets home his parents are trying the orangeade . . . "This is all I could manage!" says Mrs Bear. "We really need bigger oranges." "How's this?" says Rupert, producing Podgy's gift. "That's more like it!" nods his father. "But hasn't Mr Chimp sold out?" When Rupert explains how Podgy picked the orange from a tree, his parents are astonished. "That's very unusual in England!" says Mr Bear. "They grow in special glasshouses. There's a picture of one in this book."

"England's too cold for oranges," explains Mr Bear. "They prefer hot countries like Spain and Morocco, or the warmth of a glasshouse – like this one . . ." Rupert looks carefully at the picture in his father's book. "They were quite popular, once," continues Mr Bear. "Lots of big houses had orangeries." Rupert stares at the picture. "It looks just like Ottoline's house!" he gasps. Mr Bear looks at the picture's caption. "Nutwood Manor!" he reads. "Goodness, Rupert! You're right."

RUPERT VISITS OTTOLINE

Rupert sets out to see if he
Can find the secret orange tree . . .

"Hello, Rupert!" calls Ottoline.
"I can't believe how hot it's been!"

"We had a glasshouse, years ago,
But now there's nothing much to show . . ."

"I'd like to put it right again –
One day perhaps – I don't know when!"

As soon as he finishes lunch, Rupert decides to visit Ottoline to look at Nutwood Manor's orangery . . . "I expect it's *full* of oranges and lemons!" he smiles. "Ottoline probably gave Podgy a basket for helping her gather fruit . . ." When he arrives, Rupert finds his chum out in the garden, reading a book. "Isn't this sunshine lovely?" she smiles. "I've never known a summer last so long!" "Hello!" calls Rupert. "I've come to see if you can help me solve a mystery . . ."

When Ottoline hears about Podgy's oranges, she smiles and shakes her head. "They didn't come from *here*, I'm afraid. The orangery is abandoned. Nobody has grown fruit in it for years . . ." As the pair cross the garden, Rupert recognises the same glasshouse he saw in Mr Bear's book, but all broken and tumbling down . . . "I've always wanted to grow our own fruit," says Ottoline. "But Father says the orangery would cost too much to repair. It seems such a shame to leave it standing empty!"

"Good luck!" calls Ottoline. "Be sure
To tell me if you find out more!"

That night, Rupert tells Mrs Bear
He'd like some cooling evening air.

As Rupert sleeps, he's woken by
The sound of someone's urgent cry . . .

An Autumn Elf! "I've come to see
If you can solve a mystery!"

"Let me know if you find out any more!" calls Ottoline as Rupert sets off home. "It's exciting to think of someone growing oranges in Nutwood, though I can't think who it can be . . ." Rupert's parents can't think where the oranges have come from either. "If Podgy said he picked them, then he probably did!" says Mrs Bear. "Ask him again tomorrow." That night it is so hot that Rupert decides to sleep with his window open. "Just a little," he says. "The cool air feels delicious!"

As Rupert sleeps, he is suddenly woken by a noise at the open window . . . "Somebody's calling my name!" he thinks. "I wonder who it can be?" Sitting up in bed, he sees a shadowy figure clambering over the sill . . . "An Autumn Elf!" gasps Rupert as he recognises the little man. "Hello!" says the visitor. "Sorry to startle you, but I've been sent by the Chief Elf to ask for your help. There's something very strange going on in Nutwood. Very strange indeed . . ."

RUPERT LEARNS ABOUT A DROUGHT

"This summer there's been so much sun
The plants look as though Autumn's come!"

"Please help us, Rupert. Find out what
Has made the weather grow so hot!"

Next morning Mr Bear says, "Strange!
The dial still points to sun! No change . . ."

"The Weather Clerk should sort things out –
Or else there'll be a Nutwood drought!"

The Elf tells Rupert that Nutwood's summer heat wave is threatening to kill off next year's plants. "Everything's happening too quickly!" he complains. "Trees are shedding their leaves, flowers are dropping their petals and the grass is all scorched and dry." "Just what my father said!" nods Rupert. "It hasn't rained all summer . . ." "The Chief's stumped!" says the Elf. "Can *you* help us find out what's happening?" "I'll try!" promises Rupert. "Tell your Chief I'll do my best!"

Next morning, Rupert comes downstairs to find his father peering at the barometer. "Still no change!" he sighs. "I can't understand it! There isn't a drought in other parts of the county . . . Nutchester's just had two inches of rain! I suppose the Clerk of the Weather knows his job, but if we don't get a downpour soon, Nutwood will be a desert!" "The Clerk of the Weather!" thinks Rupert. "Of course! He's the person to sort things out. I'll send him a message straightaway . . ."

RUPERT SENDS A MESSAGE

"I'll ask the Clerk to send rain soon . . .
Just what I need – a big balloon!"

"I hope that the Weather Clerk sees,"
Thinks Rupert as he writes, "Help, Please!"

On Nutwood common, Rupert blows
The balloon till his message shows . . .

"It's working!" Rupert cries, "Hurray!"
A wind whisks the balloon away . . .

The Clerk is a kindly old man who controls the world's weather from an astonishing headquarters, up above the clouds. Rupert has met him before and is sure he will agree to help. "How can I send him a message?" he murmurs. Rummaging through his toy cupboard, he suddenly has an idea . . . "A balloon!" he cries. "I'll write a message on it, then send it up to where the Weather Clerk is bound to see!" Holding the balloon flat, he begins to write, "Weather Clerk – I need your help . . ."

As soon as the ink is dry, Rupert hurries out to the common and starts to blow up the balloon. To his delight, the writing on it grows bigger and bigger, until he is sure the Clerk will be able to read it easily. "Now all I need is a wind!" he thinks. Luckily, a breeze catches the balloon and carries it up into the sky. Rupert watches it drift higher and higher until it disappears into the clouds. "I'll wait here," he thinks. "Perhaps the Clerk will send a message back."

RUPERT MEETS THE WEATHER CLERK

As Rupert waits, a plane appears –
"The Weather Clerk's arrived!" he cheers.

"Hello!" the Clerk says. "I could read
Your message. Tell me what you need . . ."

The Clerk's amazed. "Nutwood's too dry?
They've had a drought? I can't think why . . ."

"I sent you rain clouds, let me see . . .
It should have rained quite recently!"

As Rupert waits on the common, he suddenly hears the drone of an engine. Looking up, he spots the Weather Clerk's cloud-hopper, swooping down towards him. "Hello!" calls the old man. "I got your message! Saw a balloon drifting up through the clouds, then read what it said through my strongest telescope . . ." "Thank goodness!" says Rupert. "We really need your help! Everyone in Nutwood has been complaining about too much sunshine and how we haven't had a drop of rain . . ."

The Weather Clerk is astonished by Rupert's news. "Too much sunshine?" he blinks. "I've had complaints about too much rain before, but most people like the sun." "People don't mind, it's Nutwood's plants that need water!" explains Rupert. "If it doesn't rain soon they'll all wither and die!" "But I sent rain to Nutwood!" says the Clerk. "Last week! You should have had a wet weekend." "Not a dark cloud in the sky!" says Rupert. "It's been sunny for weeks and weeks . . ."

The Clerk agrees to send more rain
Then flies off quickly in his plane . . .

Next moment, Rupert hears a call –
"Hello there! Any news at all?"

Rupert tells Ottoline that they
Should have rain soon, "It's on the way!"

"There's Podgy!" Rupert says. "Let's see
If he'll show us the orange tree . . ."

The Weather Clerk makes a note of Rupert's complaint and promises to send more rain to Nutwood at once. "I can't think what can have happened to your first batch of clouds!" he says. "It's very unusual for them to be blown so far off course . . ." No sooner has the Clerk left than Rupert hears a familiar call from the other side of the common. "Ottoline!" he cries. "Just wait till I tell you what's happened . . ." "More news?" asks his chum. "Don't say you've discovered Podgy's tree?"

Rupert tells Ottoline how he has been trying to help the Autumn Elves . . . "They're worried that this heatwave will kill off Nutwood's plants!" he explains. "Oh, dear!" says Ottoline. "I suppose they need a good, long spell of rain." "Exactly!" says Rupert. "I asked the Weather Clerk and he promised to send some straightaway." Just then, the chums spot Podgy, walking across the common with an empty basket. "Look!" says Rupert. "I wonder if he's off to gather more oranges?"

"More oranges?" laughs Podgy. "No!
I'm off to find where brambles grow . . ."

"I wonder?" Rupert says. "There's more
To this than meets the eye, I'm sure!"

The pair see where their chum's goal lies –
"The Professor's tower!" Rupert cries.

Then, suddenly, dark clouds appear.
"Hurray! At last we'll have rain here!"

Overcome with curiosity, Rupert asks his chum if he is off to pick more fruit . . . "More fruit?" laughs Podgy nervously. "Oh, oranges, you mean? There's not much chance of that! I suppose I might find some early blackberries, if I'm lucky. Bit of a wild goose chase really, but at least I'll have a good walk . . ." "How odd!" says Ottoline. "I didn't think Podgy liked walking!" "He doesn't!" smiles Rupert. "There's more to this than meets the eye! Let's follow him and see where he goes . . ."

To the chums' surprise, Podgy doesn't go far across the common, but turns off, towards the old Professor's tower . . . "I wonder what he's up to?" murmurs Rupert. "His basket's still empty, but I'm sure there aren't any fruit trees growing here!" As the pair follow Podgy, the sky above them suddenly grows darker and darker. "Rain clouds!" cries Ottoline. "Thank goodness!" cheers Rupert. "They must be from the Clerk of the Weather. He promised to put an end to Nutwood's drought."

RUPERT IS MYSTIFIED

*"Help!" Ottoline cries. "We'll both be
Wet through! Let's shelter near this tree . . ."*

*But, as the two pals watch the sky,
The clouds veer off – "I wonder why?"*

*"How odd!" says Rupert. "Not a drop!
But why? It seems the sun won't stop . . ."*

*The pair meet Bodkin, "Come this way –
Free oranges for all today!"*

The clouds above Nutwood look so dark and threatening that Rupert and Ottoline decide to take shelter. "There's going to be an absolute deluge!" says Ottoline. "We'll be lucky not to get soaked . . ." To the friends' surprise, the sky suddenly starts to clear as the rain clouds veer away from the Professor's tower. "They're moving off to Nutchester!" gasps Rupert. "I'm sure it's got something to do with the Professor. Let's go and see what he makes of this strange weather."

By the time that Rupert and Ottoline near the Professor's tower, the sky is completely clear again. "It's sunnier than ever!" shrugs Ottoline. "And we didn't have a drop of rain . . ." On the way into the garden, the pair meet the Professor's servant, Bodkin. "Hello!" he smiles. "Come in search of oranges? I asked Podgy to tell everyone in Nutwood to come and help themselves." "Oranges?" blinks Rupert. "Yes!" beams Bodkin proudly. "Plenty for all! Lots of lemons too!"

In Bodkin's garden Rupert sees
A grove of laden orange trees . . .

"So this is Podgy's secret store!"
Laughs Rupert. "Look! He's picking more!"

The pals hear the Professor call,
"Please help yourselves – there's fruit for all!"

The proud inventor says he'll show
The chums what helped the trees to grow . . .

Bodkin leads the mystified pals to a walled garden where a large sign reads, "Free oranges and lemons – please pick your own!" "Goodness!" blinks Rupert. "There isn't just *one* orange tree. There must be over twenty." "Twenty-two, if you count the lemons," smiles Bodkin. "It's been one of our most successful experiments! The only thing I can't understand is why we haven't had more visitors . . ." "I can!" says Rupert, spotting a familiar-looking figure in amongst the trees.

"I was going to tell you about the oranges, really . . ." says Podgy. "Even *I* couldn't eat all these!" "I should hope not!" beams the Professor as he joins the pals in the garden. "Plenty of oranges for everyone! It's a bumper crop!" "I'll say!" agrees Rupert. "But *how* did you manage to grow so many? I thought England was too cold and rainy for oranges and lemons?" "It is, normally!" laughs the Professor. "That's why I made my new invention. Come and see!"

RUPERT SEES A NEW INVENTION

The pals climb up, then reach a door
All wondering what lies in store . . .

"My new machine! It's guaranteed
To bring the sunshine fruit trees need!"

"My sundial sends the clouds away
And gives us sunshine every day . . ."

"I see!" gasps Rupert. "Now it's plain
Why Nutchester's had so much rain!"

Rupert is always fascinated by the Professor's inventions and can hardly wait to see his latest device. To his surprise, they go past the main laboratory and up a flight of steps that leads to the roof of the tower. "Here we are!" puffs the Professor. "Guaranteed sunshine for oranges and lemons. Just the weather they like!" "W-what is it?" asks Ottoline, staring at the strange machine. "A sundial!" says the Professor. "It's been switched on all summer . . ."

To the chums' amazement, the Professor tells them that his latest invention increases the amount of sunshine by driving off clouds . . . "You just set the dial to show how much sun you want!" he explains. "I've chosen *very* hot, to help the oranges ripen." "That's what we saw!" cries Rupert. "Those clouds over Nutchester veered away just as we arrived." "Quite so!" says the Professor. "*They* get an extra shower of rain while it stays nice and sunny here in Nutwood."

RUPERT SOLVES THE MYSTERY

"*Your sundial's made Nutwood too dry –
Without rain, all our plants will die!*"

"*Oh, dear! I didn't realise!
You're quite right!" The Professor sighs.*

"*I'll turn the sundial off, but then
I won't have oranges again . . ."*

"*Wait!" Rupert cries. "I think I know
The perfect place where they can grow!*"§

At last, Rupert knows why Nutwood has been having such a long, hot summer . . . "Your sundial has upset everything!" he tells the Professor. "Oranges like it this hot, but everything else in Nutwood has been wilting in a drought! No wonder the Clerk of the Weather was so puzzled! He kept sending rain clouds to Nutwood, but the moment they got here, your new invention drove them all away!" "Oh, dear!" gasps the Professor. "I never really thought about other plants . . ."

"What a shame!" says the Professor as he switches off the sundial. "I suppose I should have known better than to meddle with the weather! Nutwood just isn't sunny enough for oranges." "I wonder?" murmurs Rupert. "There is one place in Nutwood where your trees might grow . . ." The Professor listens carefully as Rupert tells him all about the ruined orangery at Nutwood Manor. "A splendid idea!" he smiles. "If Ottoline's parents agree, we'll start the repair work straightaway!"

RUPERT SAVES THE ORANGE TREES

The pals help Bodkin make repairs
"It's good as new now!" he declares.

The old Professor brings the trees –
"You've found the perfect home for these!"

Ottoline's mother's thrilled to see
The newly-filled orangery . . .

"This time we'll share and everyone
Can come and join us in the fun!"

When Bodkin sees the old orangery, he tells the chums that all it needs is a good clean and some fresh panes of glass . . . "It's a wonderful building!" he declares. "In the old days, it must have been full of fruit for the big house!" When everything is ready, the Professor ferries all his trees to Ottoline's house on the back of a large lorry. "My word!" he marvels. "You have done well! This is just the place to put them. Light and airy, yet nice and warm . . ."

When the last of the Professor's trees have been carried inside, Ottoline fetches her mother to come and see . . . "How wonderful!" she cries. "It's a *real* orangery again!" This time, *all* Rupert's chums are invited to come and pick oranges and lemons. "There are plenty for everyone!" laughs Ottoline. "Good!" says Podgy. "Then that must mean me as well!" "Of course!" says Rupert. "You did discover the first tree, after all!" THE END.

The two foxes play a trick on Rupert that leads to a strange journey for the little bear and a change in the weather.

RUPERT WANTS A TOBOGGAN

*Says Rupert, "Since there is no snow,
On frosty ground I'll have a go."*

*As he takes his toboggan out,
He hears Bill Badger give a shout.*

For days the weather in Nutwood has been bitterly cold. But the snow Rupert keeps hoping for does not appear. "Oh dear, this is so tiresome," he sighs. "I so want to have a go on my toboggan." Then he has an idea. He finds his Daddy who is working in the garden and says, "There's quite a lot of very slippery frost about and I wondered if I might be able to use my toboggan on it. Do you think it might work?"

Mr Bear looks doubtful: "I don't think so." Then seeing that Rupert is very keen to go tobogganing, he adds, "Still, it might be worth trying." So off scampers the little bear to find a good place to try out his idea. But he has not gone far when someone calls, "Hey, Rupert, where are you off to with that toboggan?" He turns to see his pal Bill Badger running towards him.

the SNOW PUZZLE

RUPERT MEETS THE SQUIRE

"Of course, use my estate, but, please,
Keep a lookout for my lost keys."

Says Rupert, "We must watch that hump,
Or we could have a nasty bump."

When Bill hears of Rupert's idea to toboggan on frost he says, "Mmm, it might just work. But we'll need a long downhill run to keep moving. Let's find the right sort of slope." The two pals have reached the outskirts of Nutwood when they meet the Squire. When the old gentleman hears what they plan to do he smiles and says, "Well, there are plenty of good long slopes on my estate. You're welcome to try them if you like."

He ushers the delighted pair through his gates. "You can try tobogganing here to your hearts' content," he tells them. Then as he turns to go he adds, "By the way, keep your eyes open for a bunch of my keys I dropped yesterday." The pals promise to keep a lookout. As they start uphill they see a strange hump in the grass. "Let's keep clear of that," says Rupert. "It could cause a nasty spill."

RUPERT'S CHUM TAKES A TUMBLE

They reach the top and start at last,
When something white goes flashing past.

"A snowball, Bill!" "I say, that's queer,"
Says Bill. "For no snow's fallen here!"

"Hold tight!" And Rupert pushes Bill,
Who hurtles on his way downhill.

The ride without snow's just too rough,
And Bill can't hang on tight enough.

At the top Rupert and Bill find a promising slope. Bill volunteers to go first and Rupert is about to give him a push when something white flashes past their heads. "Hey, who threw that?" yells Bill angrily and jumps off the toboggan. He is starting towards some bushes when a shout from Rupert stops him. "I say, Bill, this stuff's snow!" "Impossible!" exclaims Bill. "We've had no snow." Then he examines the white stuff Rupert has scooped up.

"You're right!" he says. "But how . . . ?" The pals puzzle over the snow and who could have thrown it. But no more appears and since there is no sign of anyone they decide to go on with the tobogganing. Rupert gives a hefty push. The toboggan races off, swaying and bumping alarmingly. Bill struggles to control it, but suddenly it hits a bump, flies into the air, overturns and poor Bill is pitched headfirst over some bushes.

"Careful!" cries Jill Frost with a frown.
"You very nearly knocked me down!"

"No snow for Nutwood this year, no!
The Weather Clerk's arranged it so."

"I think I should go home," says Bill.
"I ache all over since that spill."

"Here come more snowballs!" Rupert cries.
Jill Frost just can't believe her eyes.

As Rupert plunges into the bushes after Bill, he hears a shrill voice scolding, "Do be careful! You nearly knocked me over!" Next moment he sees his pal lying on the ground looking up at a strangely clad little person. "Why, Jack Frost!" he starts to say then he sees the newcomer is a girl. "Do you know my brother Jack?" she demands. Rupert explains that he has met Jack several times and asks how he is. "Busy elsewhere," says the girl.

"That's why I'm here doing his Nutwood job. I'm Jill Frost." "Oh, I say, are we going to have snow after all?" asks Rupert. "I'm afraid not," says Jill. "The Clerk of the Weather hasn't arranged for any for Nutwood." Just then Bill says, "I do ache after that spill. I'd best go home, I think. You stay here with Jill." And off he limps. He has hardly gone when another volley of snowballs narrowly misses Rupert and Jill.

RUPERT HEARS THE SNOW IS OLD

"Who threw those?" cries the little bear.
"I'm sure they came from over there!"

Rupert is just in time to see
The foxes dash off in high glee.

"This snow," says Jill, "is one year old!
The Weather Clerk just must be told."

"I'll take you with me, little bear."
Jill throws some powder in the air.

"Right, this time I'm going to find out who threw those snowballs!" vows Rupert and runs towards a copse from where he is sure the snowballs came. Pushing through the bushes he is just in time to see the Fox brothers, Freddy and Ferdy, dash off giggling, their arms full of snowballs. He turns back to Jill to tell her. "But where did they get snow?" he adds. "That's the mystery." "More of a mystery than you think," retorts Jill who has picked up a handful.

"This is last year's snow! I can tell. The Clerk of the Weather must be told. There's something very odd here." She thinks for a moment. "Rupert," she says, "I want you to come, too. You see, I've played so many pranks on the Clerk he mightn't believe me. He'll believe you, though." "But how . . . ?" Rupert begins. "Simple!" Jill laughs. "Lie on the toboggan. Hold tight. Right?" And she throws some powder into the air.

RUPERT RIDES THE FROSTBOW

Says Jill, "I've summoned up a gale
To take us straight there without fail."

They're swept up high and travel by
A frozen rainbow in the sky.

And as they reach the frostbow's top,
Jill warns, "Don't let that snowball drop!"

"The Weather Clerk lives down there, and
In just a moment we shall land."

"That powder is to summon a wind to take us," Jill explains. "Hark, can you hear it coming?" Rupert listens and in the distance he can hear a howling growing ever louder. Suddenly the noise is all around him and Rupert finds himself swept high into the air, still clutching his snowball. He feels much less frightened when he sees Jill flying along beside him. Now they are travelling along a sparkling band in the sky.

"It's a frozen rainbow!" shouts Jill. "A frostbow!" At the top of the frostbow Jill calls, "We shall be going down now, even faster. So hold on and don't drop that snowball!" Down, down they race, faster and faster until Rupert thinks they will never be able to stop. Then through a bank of cloud they shoot and just ahead lies a cluster of strange spires and towers. "We're here!" Jill cries. "This is where the Clerk of the Weather lives!"

RUPERT MEETS THE WEATHER MAN

Once they are down Jill leads the way
To where the Weather Clerk holds sway.

Jill's played tricks on the Clerk before,
And now he thinks she's up to more.

"Oh, please, Jill's sure that this snowball
Is truly part of last year's fall."

"Yes, this is last year's snow, all right.
By now it should have melted quite!"

Jill seems to have some strange control over the wind for at a clap of her hands it changes to a gentle breeze which wafts them both down on to a sort of terrace. Jill knows the way and, telling Rupert to leave behind his toboggan, she leads the way up a flight of stairs. It leads to a tower where the Clerk himself is working. The fussy little man's face falls when he sees Jill. "Oh, dear, not more of your tricks," he sighs. "Oh, no," says Jill.

"This is truly important. This little bear, Rupert, will tell you about it." So rather nervously Rupert launches into his story of the mysterious snowballs and how Jill said that they were last year's snow. "Oh, my!" exclaims the little man. "I suspect she is playing tricks on you, too." He agrees, however, to examine the snow, and when he does he can't believe his eyes. "It is last year's snow!" he cries. "But how has it lasted?"

RUPERT IS PROMISED SNOW

"I keep a jar of each year's snow,
But last year I forgot, you know."

"And so I'm glad of this snowball.
Now I have samples of them all."

"You do want snow? I think I can
Do that for you!" exclaims the man.

"A blizzard Nutwood's way I'll send;
As much snow as you want, young friend."

Shaking his head, the Clerk of the Weather leads the friends to a set of shelves stacked with jars. Each jar has a year marked on it. "Snow," explains the Clerk. "I have a sample of every year's snow right back to the year 1820. Every year, that is, except last year's. Strangely enough, I forgot to take a sample in time. So I'm very grateful for this lot you've brought. Now my records will be up to date."

"Rupert is very disappointed there's to be no snow in Nutwood this year," Jill breaks in. "Disappointed?" says the Clerk. "You mean you want heavy snow?" "Oh, please!" cries Rupert. "Hm," murmurs the Clerk. "I may just be in time . . ." He consults a ticker tape then leads the way to a strange wheel thing where he pulls levers and presses buttons. "There!" he says at last. "I have switched a blizzard meant for Alaska to your Nutwood. Now, quick to the launching pad!"

RUPERT AND JILL FLY BACK

"Here comes the blizzard," Jill declares,
And for their flight home she prepares.

They're both swept up and off they go,
So swift and high amid the snow.

Now Rupert's on his homeward flight,
And darkness soon gives way to light.

Then home at last and down they sweep
To land in snow so soft and deep.

Wondering what on earth is going to happen now, Rupert is hustled by Jill out of the Clerk of the Weather's workshop then through passages and up stairs, collecting Rupert's toboggan on the way. At last they reach a high platform. "We're not a moment too soon," Jill pants. "Look!" And Rupert turns to see a huge bank of dark cloud looming over them. Before the little bear realises what is happening he is swept off his feet by a howling snow storm and carried into the air,

clutching his toboggan. "Don't struggle!" cries Jill. "Just let the storm carry you along." When he does relax Rupert finds that he is really quite comfortable. But he still finds the darkness and the howling of the wind rather frightening and he is glad when it starts to grow light and he finds they are gradually dropping to earth. He gets ready for a bump but instead lands gently in deep, soft snow.

RUPERT HELPS IN A RESCUE

"Please thank the Weather Clerk for me,"
Smiles Rupert, happy as can be.

The Squire's gamekeeper tries to shift
Snow from a mound deep in a drift.

"There's someone trapped here, I'm afraid!
Lend me a hand. Here, take this spade!"

They reach a door into the mound.
In it a bunch of keys is found.

"Is this better?" laughs Jill as Rupert picks himself up. "Oh, yes!" he says. "I do hope everyone else thinks so." "They'll like it a lot more than what they were going to get," Jill says. "Frost, fog and icy winds!" Then she turns and skips away, crying, "Well, I must get on with my work!" "Thank the Clerk of the Weather for being so kind!" Rupert calls after her. Later as he makes his way homeward through the Squire's estate he sees the gamekeeper clearing snow from a mound.

"Hello, Mr Foster," Rupert says when he gets up to him. "What are you doing?" The man holds up his hand. "Listen! Can you hear voices from inside this mound?" he asks. Rupert listens hard. "Yes!" he exclaims. "Then help me dig them out!" the man cries and hands him a spade. They dig desperately and in a little while they uncover a wheelbarrow, then a low door with a bunch of keys still in it.

RUPERT SEES THE HIDDEN SNOW

"There is a sort of vault inside,"
The man says as the door swings wide.

Frozen and scared, the foxes know
They've had a narrow squeak below.

"It's full of snow, heaped on the floor!
And even on that bench there's more."

"We went for more snow for a game,
And then that awful blizzard came."

"I thought this was just a great heap of snow," Rupert exclaims. "No," the gamekeeper says as he tugs to open the door, "it's a sort of vault below a grassy mound." "Of course," Rupert thinks, "that's the bump Bill and I saw on our way up the hill." The heavy door now swings open to reveal Freddy and Ferdy Fox shaking with cold. "Br-r-rr," Ferdy shivers as they stagger out on stiff legs. "W-w-we're f-f-frozen!" Curious to see inside the strange underground room, Rupert ventures into it.

In it he sees snow heaped on the floor and on low benches too. "What's snow doing inside?" he wonders. "And why were the foxes in here?" He returns to the others in time to hear Ferdy say, "It was awful in there. We went in to get some more snow, then that blizzard came and snowed up the door." "Oh yes," Freddy wails. "It all happened so quickly we didn't have a chance to get out. And it was so dark and cold!"

RUPERT HEARS THE FOXES' TALE

"One of the bunch of keys we found
Fitted the door into this mound."

"We found the snow stored in there, so
We took some just for fun, you know."

"That was last year's snow, little bear;
The Squire stored quite a lot in there."

The man says, "You shall make amends,
And clear the Squire's drive, my friends!"

Now he is sure the foxes are not really hurt the gamekeeper holds up the bunch of keys he has taken from the door. "The Squire lost these keys yesterday," he says grimly. "And I think you two have some explaining to do." So Ferdy and Freddy tell their story. They found the keys, they say, when they were taking a shortcut through the estate. They discovered that the keys fitted the door into the mound and when they found the snow inside they took some for fun.

But when they are finished Rupert still has some questions. "Mr Foster," he begins, "Jill Frost says the snow in there is last year's snow." "True," chuckles the gamekeeper. "Been there since last winter, but that is something for the Squire to tell you about. Meanwhile these foxes are going to make amends for their pranks." Ordering the brothers to bring the wheelbarrow, he leads them off to clear the snow from the Squire's drive.

RUPERT TELLS BILL HIS STORY

As Rupert's sled speeds down the hill,
He thinks, "I know – I'll call on Bill."

Now Rupert tells his story through,
Of last year's snow and this year's too.

At home he finds the Squire is there,
Deep in a talk with Mr Bear.

"I'm glad to have my keys once more.
Now I'll explain about my store."

As he races downhill on his way home, Rupert decides to call on Bill to see how he is after his spill. Mrs Badger is clearing snow from the path when he arrives and ushers him indoors where Bill is snug in an armchair. Once Rupert is sure Bill is feeling much better and they've laid plans for tobogganing next day, he tells his chum about his adventure. "I still don't know, though, why last year's snow was stored in that underground place," he winds up.

"I shall have to ask the Squire." And strangely enough, who should be talking to Mr Bear when Rupert gets home but the Squire himself. "Ah, the Squire has something to say to you, Rupert," says Mr Bear. "I've just been talking to my gamekeeper," the Squire begins, "and he tells me you helped him rescue the foxes and, as it happens, find my keys. Thank you! Mr Foster also told me you wondered why I'd kept last year's snow. Well, I'll tell you."

RUPERT LEARNS THE SECRET

"Here is the plan in which I found
An old ice-house beneath that mound."

"I tried it out with snow, you see.
It kept it fresh indefinitely."

And now the foxes come along
To say they're sorry they've done wrong.

All is forgiven. "You shall share
Tomorrow's fun!" laughs Rupert Bear.

The Squire unrolls an old paper he is holding and lays it on the table. "Last year," he says, "I found this old plan of all the buildings in my grounds. In it I discovered that the cellar under that mound was an old ice-house. Snow and ice could be stored in it all year round so that the owner of the estate could keep things cool in warm weather. I tried it out with some of last year's snow and you've seen how fresh it still is." So at last Rupert knows the answer to the snow puzzle.

As the Squire and he walk to the gate Rupert says, "It was lucky you kept some of last year's snow." But before he can explain about the Clerk of the Weather, the two foxes appear and mumble their apologies to the Squire. "And we're sorry for throwing snowballs at you, Rupert," Ferdy says. "Oh, that doesn't matter," laughs the little bear. "You missed, anyway! I say, why not come tobogganing with us tomorrow?" THE END.

RUPERT'S MEMORY GAME

After you have read all the stories in this book, you can play Rupert's fun Memory Game! Study the pictures below. Each is part of a bigger picture you will have seen in the stories. Can you answer the questions at the bottom of the page? Afterwards, check the stories to discover if you were right.

NOW TRY TO REMEMBER . . .

1. Why is Mr Bear worried?
2. What is this man selling?
3. Where is Rupert going now?
4. Who is this? What's her name?
5. What is written on the balloon?
6. What is Rupert picking up?
7. What is Captain Barnacle making?
8. How does the Professor rescue Rupert?
9. What is in the jar?
10. What is Rupert holding carefully?
11. What is happening to Bill here?
12. Where is Rupert being taken?
13. Why does Rupert suddenly wake up?
14. What is the name of Rupert's friend?
15. Why is the Imp so upset?
16. Where is Rupert off to?

RUPERT
and the
Christmas Birds

RUPERT DOES HIS CHRISTMAS SHOPPING

*In Nutwood, Rupert's pleased to see
A splendid, festive Christmas tree.*

*They've shopped all day – just one more stop,
At Nutwood's book and paper shop.*

*Twice Rupert Bear consults their list
To check that nothing has been missed.*

*"Just what I need," says Rupert, "Look!
An origami teaching book."*

It's nearly Christmas time! When Rupert and his Mummy go into town to go Christmas shopping, they see a wonderful Christmas tree dressed with shiny baubles and a star on top. "Oh, please may we decorate our tree like that one?" Rupert asks. "Yes, we need to decorate for your Christmas party tomorrow," Mrs Bear replies. Rupert is going to invite his friends round for a Christmas tea, with games and music and mince pies. But first, they must finish up their shopping.

"I need to make invitations for my chums," Rupert remembers, as he looks down the Christmas shopping list. They stop in a small shop that sells books and paper. Rupert spots a bright orange book on the shelf – it's a book about how to fold paper into origami. "This is topping!" Rupert thinks. "It will show me how to make homemade cards, and some paper crafts and decorations as well." Mrs Bear agrees to buy the book for Rupert and then they head home together.

Once back at home, he thinks with glee,
"Tomorrow is our Christmas tea!"

"May I invite my chums, oh please?"
"Of course," says Mr Bear with ease.

"I'll make each friend a Christmas card,"
Says Rupert Bear. "It won't be hard."

And then he folds a paper bird.
He makes another . . . and a third!

While Mrs Bear unpacks her basket, Rupert takes his new book and shows it to Mr Bear. "Well, this looks clever," says Mr Bear as he flips through the pages. "What are you going to try first?" "I want to make invitations to give to my friends. Please may I invite everyone?" Rupert asks. "Yes, the more the merrier," his Daddy agrees, and so Rupert sets up at the kitchen table. The book comes with some special sheets of paper – just what he needs for Christmas invitations!

When Rupert has finished making his Christmas invitations, he still has a few sheets of the nice paper left. "Now what else can I make?" he wonders, as he turns the pages for inspiration. There! He sees the instructions for folding a paper bird. Rupert follows the directions carefully, folding it corner-to-corner, and then side-to-side. His efforts are rewarded with an attractive paper bird! Rupert is so pleased that he makes another one for his Mummy, and one for his Daddy.

His mummy cheers, "How grand they look,
That really is a clever book."

Then Rupert sees, to his delight,
The snow is falling, fast and white.

"May I go out, please?" Rupert cries.
"Yes – take your coat," his Mum replies.

He spies his chums beyond the hill –
It's Bingo, Podgy Pig and Bill.

Mrs Bear is thrilled with the small paper bird that Rupert gives her. "How clever," she marvels, and suggests that Rupert might use the birds to decorate the tree. Then their Christmas tree will be just as festive as the one they saw beautifully decorated in town! Rupert thinks this is a grand idea, but all at once his thoughts are interrupted when he glances out of the window and sees that it's starting to snow. Christmas is well and truly arriving!

"Please may I go out?" Rupert asks, and his Mummy smiles and reminds him to take his coat. "Don't forget your Christmas invitations in case you see your chums," she says. Rupert packs the cards in his satchel and carefully puts one of the paper birds on top. He can't wait to show his friends what he's made! Rupert steps outside. The snowflakes are swirling around and already there is a fine layer of snow covering the grass. "It's a good job I've got my coat!" Rupert thinks.

RUPERT SHOWS OFF HIS PAPER BIRD

His friends cry, "We're so glad you're here!
It's our first snowman of the year!"

Says Rupert, "I've made something too –
A Christmas card for each of you!"

He hands an invite to each chum.
"The tea's tomorrow. Please do come!"

Then Rupert takes his small bird out.
"A jolly thing!" the others shout.

Rupert spies his pals on Nutwood Common. He makes his way through the snow, leaving deep footprints behind. "Hello! It's Rupert!" Bingo calls out. "We're making our first snowman of the year!" "Yes, and I brought coal for the eyes and a carrot for a nose," Bill Badger adds. Rupert stops to admire the snowman, then takes the invitations out of his satchel. "Will you come to my Christmas tea tomorrow?" he asks. "I made these invitations just for you!"

"I'll be there," Podgy Pig replies. "Will there be lots of good food to eat?" he adds quickly. Rupert laughs and tells his friends about the mince pies and other Christmas nibbles. "And we'll sing Christmas songs too," Rupert says. Then he remembers the paper bird he made and takes it out to show the others. "I learned to fold this from an origami book that my Mummy bought me," he explains. "You made that yourself? It's jolly good," Bill murmers.

"Let's watch it fly," says Rupert Bear,
While tossing it into the air.

Then Rupert nearly jumps in shock,
As he's surrounded by a flock.

The birds are flying all around,
But one bird wobbles to the ground.

"A pigeon!" Rupert frowns. "Oh, my!
Her wing is hurt – she cannot fly!"

Bingo the brainy pup wants to know if the bird has the right sort of wingspan to fly. He quickly explains how paper aeroplanes work – the air that moves over and under its wings gives it lift. Perhaps Rupert's paper bird might be the same, so Rupert tosses it up, up, up into the sky. The paper bird glides gently at first. But suddenly his bird is engulfed by a flock of *real* birds, swiftly flapping their wings. "Where did these birds come from?" Rupert wonders out loud.

But before anyone can answer, one small bird near the back of the flock breaks off. She wobbles a bit and it's clear that she cannot fly anymore. The small bird heads towards the snow, landing with a small *plop!* Rupert rushes over to see. It's a pigeon and it appears as though one of her wings has been jostled. "Poor thing – she needs to rest so her wing can heal," Rupert says. He is wondering whether to take the bird to his friend the old Professor, when he hears a shout from behind.

RUPERT ENCOUNTERS THE PIGEON MAN

A man arrives quite suddenly.
"These pigeons all belong to me!"

"I train these pigeons so they know
The way home, any place they go."

The man thanks Rupert for his aid,
And lauds the paper bird he made.

"My master has a son your age
He'd love to see this bird, I'd wage."

"Hello! Is that one of my birds?" Rupert hears. He turns around and sees a tall man in a thick overcoat. "My name is Wilfred Wingman," the man begins. "I train carrier pigeons, so everyone just calls me the Pigeon Man." "I'm Rupert Bear, and I think this bird is injured," Rupert hastily explains. The Pigeon Man takes the bird from Rupert. "Nothing is broken, just bruised," he says, looking relieved. "I'll take her home to rest and she'll be right as rain before you know it."

Rupert is very glad to hear that. The Pigeon Man tells Rupert and his chums about his master, who is a great explorer. "His voyages take him all over the world and these pigeons carry messages back for him." When Rupert shows his new friend the paper bird he made, the Pigeon Man gets very excited. "The Explorer has a son called Marco, about your age. He's a clever boy who would love to see your paper birds. Would you like to make his acquaintance?"

RUPERT TRAVELS TO A GRAND HOUSE

As Rupert rides his new friend's sled,
He tells him of the book he read.

Across the snow and up a drive,
Then at a grand house, they arrive.

"We're pleased to meet you, Rupert Bear!
Do come inside, it's warm in there!"

The kindly bird man waves good-bye,
As Rupert goes in where it's dry.

Rupert is keen to come along. His chums need to go home, but they're looking forward to the Christmas party tomorrow. Rupert hops on to the front of the Pigeon Man's sledge. He makes himself comfortable and tells the Pigeon Man all about his origami book. The sledge runners cut through the snow brilliantly and in what feels like no time at all, they reach their destination. The grand, wooden gate slides open and the Pigeon Man pushes the sledge up a long drive.

The Pigeon Man knocks on the door, which opens at once. Out steps the Explorer, followed by his son. "How kind of you to drop by," the Explorer greets them, "we were just making a pot of hot cocoa. Do come inside from the snow and warm up!" Marco grins at Rupert, and Rupert knows that they shall get along brilliantly. The Pigeon Man can't stay for long, but he introduces Rupert and tells of his paper birds. Then he waves goodbye before going on his merry way.

RUPERT MEETS THE EXPLORER AND HIS SON

The house is filled, from wall to wall,
With travel relics, big and small.

The tall explorer beams with pride,
"My journeys take me far and wide."

His new friend, Marco, cries, "I say,
Let's make some paper birds today."

"There's lots of paper – I know where
We'll find it!" he tells Rupert Bear.

When Rupert enters the Explorer's house, he can hardly believe his eyes. The walls and ceilings are covered with relics from the Explorer's travels – giant clay vases, sparkling jewels, a coat of armour and a giant stuffed bird on the ceiling. "How splendid! It's rather like a museum!" Rupert tells Marco. The Explorer brings a tray of steaming hot cocoa and starts to tell Rupert and Marco stories about the strange lands he's visited and the adventures he's had.

Rupert is thoroughly enjoying the Explorer's tales, but after they've finished the hot cocoa, Marco asks Rupert about the origami bird. Rupert takes out his book again, and Marco has an idea. "If you show me how to fold paper birds, I can help you and we can make more together." "Yes, that sounds topping," Rupert agrees. Marco shows Rupert upstairs – there's a spare room in the back of the house where they can find paper and other crafting supplies. Rupert follows eagerly.

RUPERT FOLDS A FLOCK OF PAPER BIRDS

The paper in the dusty chest
Is gleaming – Rupert is impressed.

They take it out, though neither knows,
Just why the lustrous paper glows.

First Rupert shows off how to fold
Precisely as the book has told.

"I am so pleased you taught me how,"
Cheers Marco. "We've so many, now!"

Marco pokes through a dusty old chest in the back room. Rupert tries not to sneeze as the dust goes everywhere! The top drawers only hold shells and feathers, but they're in luck, for the next drawer that Marco opens is full of bright, shiny paper. "I say, that's very unusual paper," Rupert muses. "It's almost as if the paper is *glowing*!" "I believe you're right!" Marco nods. "It must be from one of Father's journeys. The birds will look fantastic when we're finished."

Rupert opens the book to the page he used earlier. "I think I can remember how," he says, "but let's look at the instructions, just in case." Rupert shows Marco how to fold, corner-to-corner, then side-to-side. Marco is a quick learner and soon the pals have developed a rhythm. While they work, Marco tells Rupert about travelling with his father and Rupert tells Marco about his family and friends. "You must come to my Christmas tea tomorrow," he adds.

RUPERT MARVELS AS THE BIRDS COME TO LIFE

*"Your origami birds will be
Quite perfect for the Christmas tree."*

*They hang the paper birds with care,
As Christmas carols fill the air.*

*The jolly Christmas music brings,
The birds to life! They beat their wings!*

*The friends cannot believe their eyes,
As each bird flutters, flaps and flies.*

Soon, the two have made quite a pile of birds and Marco finds an empty basket to carry the birds as they walk back downstairs. The Explorer smiles to see their work. "A jolly good afternoon you've had!" he says. He is particularly bemused by the fact the birds are glowing and suggests that they go on the Christmas tree in the middle of the room. While Rupert and Marco hang the birds, the Explorer takes out his gramophone to play some of his best Christmas carols.

All at once, the paper birds appear to come to life! Each bird hovers above the tree and then, without warning, starts flapping its tiny paper wings. "Oh my, whatever is happening?" the Explorer gasps. Before anyone can answer, the birds are fluttering around the room. They swoop over the tree, under the ladder, past the gramophone and towards the window! "What shall we do?" cries Rupert. "I'll close the window," Marco replies . . . but it's too late!

RUPERT LEARNS THE PAPER IS MAGIC

And then outside the bright birds fly,
They shimmer in the winter sky.

The music stops. The birds look round,
Then slowly topple to the ground.

The glowing paper! Could it be
It made the birds fly merrily?

"Enchanted paper? Most absurd!"
They marvel, picking up each bird.

The paper birds have flown out of the window. "They could be flying *anywhere*!" Rupert says. "We'll never get them back!" Marco laments. But Rupert jumps in place. "Wait! I have an idea," he calls. "If it was the Christmas music that brought these birds to life, perhaps we can reverse it before it's too late!" So the Explorer turns off the gramophone at once. As the music fades, the paper birds slowly fold up their wings and drift to the ground.

"That was quick thinking," the Explorer tells Rupert. "Yes, but how did the birds come to life in the first place?" Rupert wants to know. "I think I can guess," the Explorer says. "I've had the glowing paper for so long, I'd nearly forgotten about it! Many years ago, it was given to me on my travels. I was told that it was enchanted paper, but I never knew what the enchantment was. Now I know that *music* is the key!" "We might as well collect the paper birds now," Marco suggests.

"It's getting late and I must go,"
Says Rupert, dressing for the snow.

"The magic birds – you should take half,"
Says Marco, with a cheery laugh.

It's been a thrilling afternoon,
And Rupert hurries home quite soon.

"We're glad you're home," his parents say.
"Do tell us all about your day!"

With the paper birds back in the basket, Rupert realises that it's time for him to go home now. It's still snowing outside, so he wraps up in his coat and scarf. "I've had a lovely afternoon," says Marco. "Yes, I have too – and see you tomorrow at my Christmas party!" Rupert replies. Then Marco winks and whispers, "We made these magic birds together, so you should take half of them." And he puts some of the origami birds into a box for Rupert to take home with him.

It's getting colder, but Rupert hurries home and arrives just in time for tea! "There you are," says Mrs Bear. "How was your day?" "Oh my," Rupert laughs. "I'm not sure you'd believe me if I told you!" Over dinner, Rupert starts to tell about building a snowman with his friends and the Pigeon Man and the Explorer and Marco . . . but before he can finish his story, it's time for bed. "Tomorrow will be a great party," Rupert thinks as he drifts off to sleep.

When morning comes, he's quickly stirred,
Remembering each magic bird.

"My party's soon! I cannot wait –
I'll use these birds to decorate."

He takes the paper birds with glee,
And gently sits them on the tree.

His chums arrive and Rupert's glad,
That Marco comes and brings his Dad.

In the morning, Rupert wakes up and rubs his eyes. Then he remembers that today is his Christmas tea! "I'd better get up and start to get ready!" he thinks. Then he remembers the package Marco gave him last night. Inside are the paper birds, still glowing. Rupert grins as he thinks about the fun he will have today. "You seem very excited, Rupert," says Mrs Bear. She and Mr Bear are tidying the house, so nobody notices as Rupert puts the glowing birds on the Christmas tree.

Soon, Rupert's chums start to arrive. "Hello, Bill! Hello, Podgy Pig! Hello Bingo!" Rupert calls. "Hello, hello!" they reply. "And a very happy Christmas to you!" Bill Badger adds. And Rupert is delighted to see that Marco and the Explorer have come as well. He introduces them to his friends and before long, Rupert's chums are gathered around the Explorer while he tells marvellous tales about a Christmas expedition he went on many years ago.

RUPERT WISHES EVERYONE A HAPPY CHRISTMAS

When Marco sees the tree, he blinks,
Then grins at Rupert, as he winks.

Soon everyone has come along –
It's time to play a Christmas song.

And with the music playing loud,
The magic birds astound the crowd.

They beat their wings, and Rupert cries,
"A Happy Christmas and . . . SURPRISE!"

While the others are listening to the Explorer's stories, Marco gets up to admire Rupert's Christmas tree. His eyes grow wide when he recognises the shimmering paper birds from the day before. Rupert smiles and Marco winks again. Then Mr Bear says, "Shall we have some jolly Christmas tunes?" "Yes, yes!" the others cheer. Mr Bear sets up the gramophone and turns it on. Soon, Christmas music fills the room and Rupert's chums sing along.

And then, just as Rupert has expected . . . the birds come to life again! They flutter merrily around the room, sparkling like Christmas candles. "Again?" gasps the Explorer. "Oh, my!" cries Mrs Bear. "What fun!" adds Mr Bear. "This is the best Christmas surprise!" Bill pipes up. Rupert and Marco grin at each other as everyone in the room marvels at the magical Christmas birds. "Happy Christmas to everyone!" Rupert shouts. "And surprise!" THE END.

Spot the Difference

Rupert's magical birds are out on this cold winter's day, flying with a whole host of birds. There are 10 differences between the two pictures. Can you spot them all?

Answers: Rupert's waving hand is missing, the little cottage has changed colour, the parrot's colours have also changed, Bill Badger has been replaced with Algy Pup, Bingo Pup's scarf is now blue, two of the paper birds are now a real birds, one of the orange paper birds is flying in the other direction, a green paper bird is now blue and one of the real birds is missing.

HOW TO MAKE A PAPER BIRD

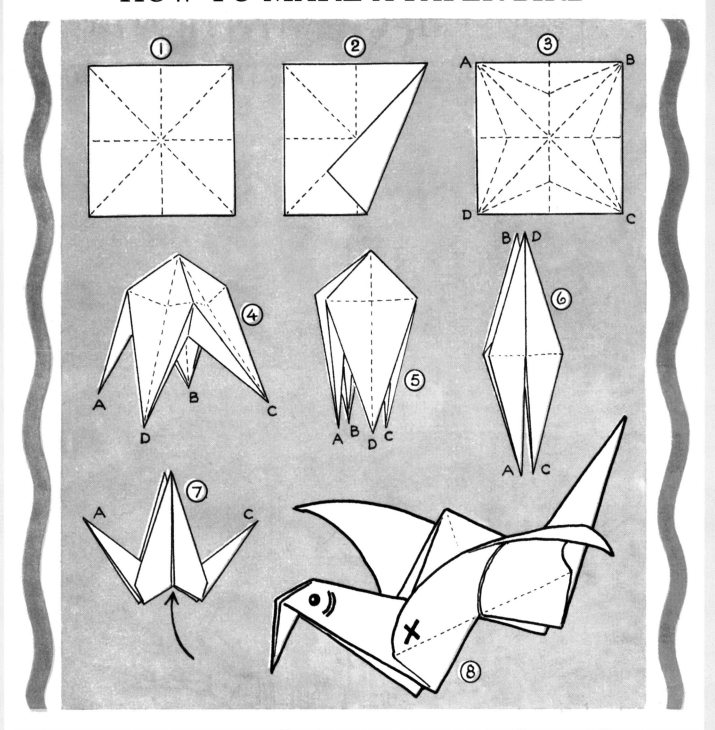

Do you know how to make a paper bird like the one Rupert made in the last story?

Take a perfectly square piece of paper and fold it from corner to corner each way. Then turn it over and fold it from side to side as in (1). Next lay each side against a middle line (2) but press the fold only half-way along from the corner. Do this all round until the pattern of the folds looks like (3). Now press the four side panels under and, working by the folds you have made, gently bring the corners together as in (4) and (5). When A, B, C and D are tight together press everything firmly into its new position.

Next lift the opposing flaps B and D. These will be the wings (6). Now comes a tricky bit as you lift A and C to a half-way position as shown in (7). The folds at the point marked by an arrow must be neat and careful, and the paper must not tear. For the finishing touches fold down the tip of A to form the beak and draw in an eye. Lastly, take each wing and gently bend it outwards into a curve as in (8) – this is necessary or the bird won't "work".

To make it flap its wings, hold the bird at the point marked X (not lower) and gently pull its tail!

If you glue on a string, your paper bird can be hung nicely on a Christmas tree.

RUPERT'S CHRISTMAS DECORATIONS

Your Christmas tree will look very pretty if you follow Rupert's idea of making your own decorations. Candles, lanterns, baby crackers and other festive things can be made from oddments which you will find in the house.

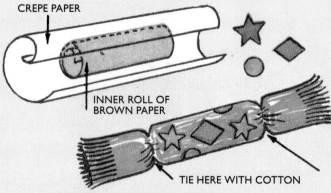

CREPE PAPER

INNER ROLL OF BROWN PAPER

TIE HERE WITH COTTON

BUTTON

SILK TASSEL

Baby Cracker: Roll a strip of brown paper into a thin tube 2 inches long and glue the outer edge to keep the paper from unrolling. Cover the tube with a piece of coloured crepe paper which should overlap the tube about 1 inch at each end – a touch of glue will keep the outer covering firm. Make the "waists" of the cracker by fastening cotton just beyond the ends of the inner tube. Cut fringes at the edges, then decorate the cracker with tiny shapes of coloured paper cut from sweet-wrappers.

Dwarf Lantern: Cut four pieces of paper 4.5 inches by 1.5 inches and two pieces of card 2 inches square. Colour the strips of paper and pleat them. Make a tassel with short lengths of silk thread, and fasten it through the middle of one piece of card. Sew the buttons to the centre of the other card, leaving a loop to attach to the tree. Paste the ends of your pleated papers to the cards to form the walls of the lanterns.

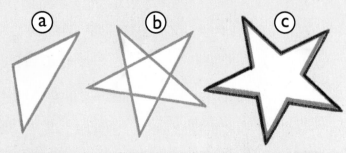

(a) (b) (c)

Tree Tassel: Fold three or four coloured sweet-wrappers together to make a narrow strip, then fold the strip in half and fasten the loop of thread round the folded part. Snip the ends to form a fringe which can be spread out, as shown.

Tree-top Star: Make a card triangle about three times the size of that shown in figure (a). Cut it out and use it as a pattern. Place it on a piece of card and draw round it in three different positions so that you draw figure (b). Now cut round the outer lines shown black in figure (c). To decorate the star, you can either paint it a bright yellow or glue silver paper onto it. Tape a loop of paper to the back of the star so that it can be hung on your tree.

COCKTAIL STICK

LOOP OF THREAD

BEAD

Sparklers: Find five coloured metal milk-bottle or cola-bottle tops and make a small hole in the centre of each. Push a cocktail stick through the holes, as shown, and fix each top with a drop of glue. Hang the sparklers on your tree and they will glitter in the light.

Elfin Bell: A metal milk-bottle top can be made to the shape of a bell by moulding it on a thimble. Remove the thimble and trim the edges of the bell. Thread a small bead and sew it inside the bell as shown, leaving a loop of thread at the top.

COCKTAIL STICK

PAPER TUBE

MILK BOTTLE TOP

COTTON WOOL

FINISHED CANDLE AND HOLDER

Fairy Candle: Push some cotton-wool in the end of a thin paper tube about 1.5 inches long. Glue the wool in position and twist one end to form a "wick". Fit a cocktail stick through the centre of a milk bottle top, as shown, and glue it into the cotton-wool.

SHAPES GUMMED BACK TO BACK ON THREAD

Paper Chains: Some small coloured paper shapes are glued back-to-back on a length of thread. When draped on your tree these chains will look very jolly.

Rupert
and the
Goblin Cobbler

Rupert
buys his mother a
Christmas present
and makes her
dance

Says Rupert, "Here's my Christmas list!
Has anyone, Mamma, been missed?"

Then when they're sure the list is right
They set out for the shops so bright.

First, lots of presents Rupert buys,
Then, "Go home, Mummy, please," he cries.

He wants to find a gift for her,
And sees some slippers lined with fur.

Christmas is very near and Rupert is deep in the problem of making a list of the presents he is going to give to his friends. Mrs Bear looks on and tries to help him in his choice. At last they agree that the list is complete, and together they set off through the snow to the nearest town where the bright shops are displaying all the Christmas gifts.

They have a merry time buying the presents and Mrs Bear puts them into her basket. Then Rupert asks her if she will start for home and he will follow as soon as he can, as he has one more important present to get. Mrs Bear agrees, but tells Rupert not to be late home. As soon as she is out of sight Rupert goes to buy a surprise present for his mother.

He says, "I'd like those slippers, please,
For Mummy's chilblains they will ease."

Then home he trudges through the snow,
And hears a frightened voice cry, "Oh!"

There's someone buried in the drift,
And Rupert tries the snow to shift.

At Granny Trunk's he calls for aid;
She says, "Dear me, I'll fetch my spade."

Rupert sees a lovely pair of warm slippers in the shop. "Just the thing for mummy," he thinks, and buys them, "they will comfort her chilblains." Happily he sets out over the snow towards his home. His way lies by a snowdrift and suddenly he stops and listens. A voice seems to be calling for help out of the middle of the drift.

Thinking someone is buried in the snowdrift Rupert starts to scoop away the snow, but the drift is too deep for him, so he runs for help to the nearest cottage. "That is very extraordinary," says Granny Trunk when she has listened in astonishment to Rupert's story. "I'm too old to go with you, my dear, but I can lend you a spade if you like."

Now Rupert starts the snow to explore
And in a tree he finds a door.

Out pops a funny little man,
Shut in there since the snow began.

"I make," he says, "All kinds of shoe;
Now how, my lad, can I help you?"

So Rupert says, "Just tell me, please,
If these warm shoes chilblains will ease."

With the spade Rupert makes short work of boring into the snowdrift and he is amazed to find that the voice is coming from behind a door leading right into a great tree. When he has cleared a passage the door flies open and the queerest little man pops out. "Thank you!" he cries. "I was losing all my trade, I couldn't get out and my customers couldn't get in!" "But who are you?" gasps Rupert.

"Don't you know me?" says the little man, "I'm a goblin cobbler. Now what can I do to repay you for setting me free from the snowdrift?" "Nothing at all," says Rupert, "but I wish you would tell me if these are really good slippers. I've bought them for mother because of her chilblains." "Aha," chuckles the little cobbler. "Come into my workshop, I can help you."

RUPERT LEAVES THE COBBLER

The goblin says, "In these I'll drop
Some chilblain powder from my shop."

Then Rupert thanks the little gnome,
And once more gaily starts for home.

"Oh, thank you, dear," says Mrs Bear,
"What lovely shoes for me to wear!"

But when they're on she can't keep still,
And dances till she feels quite ill.

Rupert watches in surprise as the goblin cobbler takes a glass jar from a shelf and sprinkles a little powder in each of the slippers. "There," says the little fellow, "that is goblin chilblain powder, and your mother will never suffer from them again once she has worn these slippers." Rupert is delighted, thanks the cobbler and leaves for home. "Come and see me again," shouts the goblin as he waves good-bye.

Mrs Bear is surprised and very pleased with her present and hurries to try on the slippers. "They are very comfortable, indeed," she says, and Rupert smiles to himself as he thinks of the goblin cobbler's words, but his expression soon changes, for his mother suddenly looks anxious and starts dancing about. "This is very queer," she says, "I can't keep my feet still."

RUPERT RUNS FOR HELP

Now Rupert sees that something's wrong
And fetches Mr Bear along.

Then off he runs with all his might
To ask his friend to put things right.

The goblin cobbler starts to quake;
"I've made," he says, "a bad mistake."

A powder jar he grabs in haste.
"Come quick!" he cries, "no time to waste."

Realising that something has gone wrong with his plans Rupert runs to find his father. When they return they find Mrs Bear still dancing round the room as though she can't stop. Losing no more time Rupert snatches up his scarf and runs full speed back to the cobbler and finds his friend standing near his tree.

The goblin cobbler listens in dismay while Rupert tells his story. "Oh, dear!" he moans, "I must have made a mistake and used the wrong powder. Come on – we've no time to lose," and he runs into his workshop for another jar of powder. Then grabbing Rupert by the arm he sets off at a surprising rate for Nutwood.

RUPERT LOSES HIS FRIEND

"I've kicked them off," wails Mrs Bear,
"I danced till I was in despair."

"Allow me to apologise
And make them right," the gnome replies.

The cobbler says, "Please, I implore,
Try on the powdered shoes once more."

But when at last she has them on,
To their surprise the gnome has gone!

Rupert and the goblin cobbler find that Mrs Bear has managed to kick off the slippers and she and Mr Bear look in great surprise at Rupert's queer little friend. "It's as I thought," says the goblin. "I used dancing powder by mistake!" Shaking the slippers thoroughly he sprinkles them with the new powder. "There," he says, "now you'll never have chilblains again!"

After her recent experience Mrs Bear hesitates to put the slippers on again, but at last she screws up courage. "Why, they're lovely," she smiles. "Thank you, Rupert dear, I never felt so comfy." Then they all turn to thank the goblin cobbler for his share in cobbler present. To their amazement he isn't there at all. "Well, you do find some strange friends, Rupert," says Mrs Bear. THE END.

FOLLOW
RUPERT
EVERY
MORNING
IN THE
DAILY
EXPRESS

From the
Rupert Annual,
1948